For my father, Robert, who grew up during
the Second World War, and my mother,
Ruth, who was born in the middle of it.

First published in the UK in 2023 by Nosy Crow Ltd
Wheat Wharf, 27a Shad Thames,
London, SE1 2XZ, UK

Nosy Crow Eireann Ltd
44 Orchard Grove, Kenmare,
Co Kerry, V93 FY22, Ireland

ISBN: 978 1 78800 464 0

A CIP catalogue record for this book will be available from
the British Library.

Printed and bound in Great Britain by Clays Ltd, Elcograf S.p.A.
Typeset by Tiger Media

Papers used by Nosy Crow are made from wood grown in
sustainable forests.

MIX
Paper from
responsible sources
FSC® C018072

1 2 3 4 5 6 7 8 9 10

www.nosycrow.com

# CHAPTER ONE

# Right in the Middle
# of the Chaos

Nancy gaped at the enormous mansion in the distance. *Oh my giddy aunt*, she thought. That's not a house. It's a palace.

Her stomach squirmed as she stood at the bend in the drive, clutching her little cardboard suitcase. How would she ever fit in here?

She took a deep breath. *You'll be fine*, she told herself. *Mother did it. Granny did it. And it's not as if you've never cleaned a house before.*

But *this* house?

Nancy had an overwhelming urge to run back to the station and catch the next train home. But she made herself keep walking.

As she rounded the bend, she saw that the house formed three sides of a massive square, set around a huge courtyard. And every inch of the courtyard was littered with school desks, chairs, pianos, mattresses, music stands, bed frames, easels, tables, boxes and packing cases. It looked as though a mischievous god had picked up a school building, dangled it above the house and emptied its contents on to the grass.

As she stared at the scene, a boy about her own age, in a flat cap several sizes too big for him, swaggered out of the main entrance. He grinned at Nancy.

"Hey, redhead! Watch out, your hair's on fire!"

She rolled her eyes. "Very funny. Never heard that one before."

"Nancy!" said a voice behind her.

She turned and saw a man in a chauffeur's uniform carrying a packing case. What a relief to see a familiar face.

"Oh, hello, Mr Burford," she said.

"Hello, Nancy. How was your journey?" he asked, setting down the case and wiping his sweaty brow with a handkerchief.

"Not too bad, thank you. The train was packed with soldiers and evacuees, though."

"Seems like the whole country's on the move since Hitler reached the French coast," Mr Burford said. He beckoned to the boy to come and join them. "This is Albert. He helps out in the gardens and stables. Nancy's the new housemaid, Albert."

The boy nodded to Nancy and she raised her eyebrows with a look that said, *Not so cheeky now your boss is here, are you?* She noticed that he only had one arm. His right shirtsleeve was tucked into his belt.

"I'm afraid you've arrived right in the middle of the chaos, Nancy," Mr Burford said.

"Yes, what's going on?"

"Girls' school, moving from the Sussex coast in case Hitler invades. We only found out on Friday."

Nancy's eyes widened. "A whole school? Will I have to clean for them too?"

Mr Burford laughed. "No, they're bringing all their own staff."

*Thank goodness for that*, Nancy thought. If she had to skivvy for a school too, she'd pretty soon be looking for another job.

"The removal men were meant to take the furniture indoors," Mr Burford said, "but they had to go and evacuate another school. You'll have to pitch in straight away, I'm afraid. Lucky you came in uniform."

"Yes, thank you for sending it. And for getting me the job."

"Well, they wanted a good strong country girl, and I thought you'd be ideal. Your mum said you won a scholarship to the grammar school, but it's better to be out at work, eh? Not much point getting a fancy education with the world as it is at the moment."

"No," said Nancy. "Anyway, I've always wanted to travel."

He laughed. "Stanbrook's not exactly Timbuktu. You've only moved twenty miles."

"It's the furthest I've ever been. And one day I'll go further."

Nobody knew how disappointed Nancy was that she'd had to leave school on her fourteenth birthday. She had told her parents she didn't mind, because what was the point in being upset? The scholarship didn't include the expensive uniform or the books, so that was that.

"How's your dad these days?" Mr Burford asked.

"Not so bad, thank you." She tried not to think about Dad's terrible coughing fit this morning. His lungs had never been right since he had been gassed in the last war.

An older girl in a green dress like Nancy's walked up a stone staircase from the basement and picked her way through the furniture towards them.

"Rosa, this is Nancy," said Mr Burford. "Nancy, this is Rosa, the head housemaid. She's an evacuee of sorts. Came over from Austria two years ago."

Rosa smiled at Nancy. "Pleased to meet you," she said. She had a slight accent, and her pale, anxious-looking face was framed by long dark plaits pinned up on her head. Nancy tried not to stare as she said hello, but she wondered why Rosa had left Austria and where the rest of her family were.

"You two take the dining tables in," Mr Burford said. "Albert and I will make a start on the beds."

As Nancy followed Rosa to a cluster of tables, a gleaming green sports car came speeding up the drive.

"Oh!" breathed Nancy. "Look at that!"

"That's Lord Evesham's car," said Rosa. "I'm sure he wasn't expected today."

"Albert, fetch Mr Armitage," called the chauffeur, straightening his cap and heading down the steps to the forecourt. "Rosa, Nancy, stand by the main entrance to greet his lordship."

From their position by the front steps, Nancy watched, entranced, as the car came to a screeching halt. "A BMW 328. Oh, my goodness! It's even more beautiful than in the photographs."

Mr Burford opened the driver's door and saluted. A tall, immaculately dressed man in a trilby sprang out of the car and glared at the furniture-strewn courtyard.

"Armitage!" he barked.

A smartly suited man appeared as if by magic, gliding across the courtyard so elegantly that you could almost have imagined the furniture was parting to make way for him.

"That's the butler," Rosa murmured.

"Welcome back, my lord," said the butler with a bow.

"What the devil is all this junk, Armitage?" said the earl. "It looks like a Boy Scouts' jumble sale."

"It is unfortunate, my lord, that you should have arrived at a time of some upheaval, but, rest assured, it will all be cleared by nightfall."

"Nightfall's no bally good to me, Armitage. I've got several vanloads of priceless porcelain arriving any minute. Get the servants to clear a path, and look sharp about it."

"Curtsy as his lordship passes," Rosa whispered.

Lord Evesham completely ignored the maids, but Mr Armitage, following him, stopped and said, "Move those tables inside quickly, then start on the chairs. The headmistress will show you where to place them." He glanced at Nancy. "You must be the new housemaid. Good."

*Some welcome*, thought Nancy. Still, you couldn't

blame him for being a bit tense. Lord Evesham didn't seem like the most easy-going employer.

As she and Rosa headed back to the tables, a fabulous red sports car pulled up on the forecourt. Nancy's mouth dropped open. A Jaguar SS100! This place really was a whole new world.

She gazed in admiration as Mr Burford opened the door. The driver got out and removed her cap, goggles and gloves.

Nancy gasped. It couldn't really be her, could it?

"What is it?" asked Rosa, grasping one end of a table.

Nancy stared at the trouser-suited woman. "Oh my giddy aunt, it's Dorothy Taylor."

"Do you know Miss Taylor?" asked Rosa.

"Of course I do," said Nancy. "I mean, I don't *know* her, but I know everything about her. Is she a friend of Lord Evesham's?"

"Yes," said Rosa. "I think she is a racing-car driver?"

"She's an *incredible* racing-car driver," said Nancy. "She beat all the men at Brooklands last year in *that* Jaguar. She races motorcycles and flies planes too. She's *amazing*. Oh, wait until I tell Jack!"

"Jack?"

"My brother. He's with the British Expeditionary Force," Nancy said with that mixture of pride and fear she always felt when she thought of Jack fighting in Europe. "He loves racing too – we used to read all the race reports together, and he's going to take me to Brooklands one day."

They heaved the table into a marble-floored entrance hall that was quite a lot bigger than Nancy's entire house. A woman who was surely the headmistress stood in the hall like a column of steel-grey tweed.

"Take that into the dining room and place it at the far end on the left," she said.

They staggered into the grandest room Nancy had ever seen. Vast oil paintings in gilt frames hung on red-silk-covered walls. A huge crystal chandelier was suspended from the ornate ceiling.

"It took eight men to move out his lordship's dining table yesterday," Rosa said.

"Where is it now?" Nancy asked.

"In the library." Rosa gestured to a door on the other side of the hall. "That will be the earl's dining room while the school is here."

As they walked back through the room, Nancy saw Lord Evesham and Dorothy Taylor in the entrance hall. Mr Armitage stood at a respectful distance.

Nancy gazed at the impossibly glamorous woman in her elegant trouser suit. She still couldn't believe her heroine was actually here.

"Do you think I could ask her for her autograph?" she whispered to Rosa.

"Her what?"

"To write her name on a piece of paper for me."

"No!" whispered Rosa, looking shocked. "You must never speak to the family or their guests unless they speak to you first."

They couldn't get out of the dining room, as the

headmistress was hovering in the doorway while the butler introduced her to Lord Evesham. Nancy watched in amusement as she blushed and bobbed a curtsy.

Lord Evesham smiled graciously. "Delighted to meet you, Miss Hathersage. Welcome to Stanbrook."

"Thank you so much, your lordship. I cannot express how much we appreciate your kindness."

"Not at all, not at all. We must all do our bit for the war effort, eh?"

The headmistress gushed a reply, but he was already walking away, with Dorothy Taylor beside him. Miss Hathersage turned to the maids. "Fetch the classroom lists from the desk in my study," she said to Rosa. "It's the Green Drawing Room, on the first floor."

"Yes, ma'am," said Rosa, and headed down the hall.

"Well, don't idle about," the headmistress said to Nancy. "Go and fetch some dining chairs."

"Yes, ma'am," said Nancy. *Bossy old bat*, she thought.

On her way out, she glimpsed Lord Evesham and Miss Taylor turning off the main corridor. Her heartbeat sped up. What if she *could* get Dorothy Taylor's autograph? Imagine sending it to Jack! Wouldn't he be amazed!

Boxes sat piled up by the front door. On some impulse, Nancy picked one up and followed the pair at a distance. They walked into a room near the end of the corridor. Nancy slowed her pace as she approached.

The door was slightly ajar, and she heard Lord Evesham say in a low voice, "We can't discuss this now. Too many people around, what with this dratted school turning up."

"Well, I don't know how else we can discuss it," said Miss Taylor. "We can't say anything on the telephone, and you might not be in London for weeks."

"Keep your voice down," he said. There was a pause, and the sound of a match being struck. "All this waiting is jarring my nerves."

"Well, Saturday is all in hand," said Miss Taylor. "So there's no need to fret where that's concerned."

"I'm still not sure you should be doing it yourself," said Lord Evesham. The smell of cigarette smoke drifted into the corridor.

"I've done far more dangerous things, Gerald. In any case, there's no risk. I've had the place watched for weeks and there's never any guard at the side gate."

"Don't take your own car," he said. "It's far too recognisable."

"Of course I won't. What sort of fool do you take me for?"

A door opened nearby and Nancy hurried on, her heart thumping and a queasy sensation in her stomach. She had no idea what they'd been talking about. But there was something about the tone and the secrecy of it that made her feel extremely uneasy.

# Sidney to George

A train
Somewhere between London and Stanbrook
27<sup>th</sup> May 1940

Dear Dordy,

Oh, goodness, your last letter was so hilare it made me snort milk through my nose at the breakfast table. I can't *believe* Douglas said that to the wing commander – will he be court-martialled or don't they do that in the Air Force?

Well, you *will* be surprised to get another letter so soon, but the fact is I'm stuck in a compartment with the vilest girl in the land, poor me, so I'm pretending to work on an English essay. Of course, now she thinks I'm the most terrific swot, but the good thing is she has absolutely no interest in what I'm writing. If Miss Verney finds out I've been using my English book for letter-writing, I'll probably be expelled, so just think of the heroic risk I'm taking for your entertainment.

How are you? Are you being terribly brave, shooting enemy planes out of the sky and doing victory rolls all day long? Everybody here thinks I'm awfully lucky to have a brother in the RAF. Of course I don't tell them you spend most of your time drinking whisky in the officers' mess. It all sounds terrific fun, lucky you.

We were early to the station, since Mother as usual was terrified of being late, so I beetled into an empty compartment and snaffled the corner seat. I was

10

thinking how well I'd done, when – horrors!! – Lucinda and Ginny and Phyllis came waltzing along the corridor, and beastly Lucinda looked in and said, "Oh, good, an empty compartment." Then she barged in and banged my shoulder with the corner of her bag as she swung it up on to the luggage rack, the little brute.

Ginny did actually say hello to me, and Phyllis looked as though she might have liked to, but she's such a frightened rabbit, she never dares so much as breathe without Lucinda's permission, so she didn't say a word. Lucinda terrifies everyone with that vicious tongue of hers.

I do think it was terribly thoughtless of the parents to send me to a new school in the summer term, it's practically impossible to make friends, everyone's in their little gangs already, but that's just typical of Pa – one word from the admiral about what a splendid place it is and how happy his daughters were at St Olave's, and his mind's made up. Did you loathe St Thomas's at first? Do tell.

It was heaven having time at home while the teachers packed up the school – I managed to read five detective stories! I've brought *The Murder of Roger Ackroyd* to Stanbrook. Did you know we're only allowed to bring one book – the utter cruelty of this place! Were they that barbaric at St Thomas's?

I'm excited to see Stanbrook. Vanessa in the Upper Fifth has visited and says it's heaven. The house is four hundred years old, so it's bound to be absolutely heaving with ghosts. I shall be utterly crushed if I don't bump into headless knights in suits of armour every time I turn a corner. Do you remember that story I wrote where all the portraits came alive and followed the children around, and you were too petrified to go into the drawing room for months in case Great-Grandfather Dashworth leaped out of his frame? Oh, I do miss you, Dordy. Take good care of yourself in that Spitfire, won't you?

Must go now as mistresses in terrific panic about gathering belongings, etc. Will send regular updates on headless knights.

Best love from your little sis

# CHAPTER TWO

# In a Neat and Seemly Line

The coach turned off the lane and trundled up a long drive through a vast green park dotted with enormous trees. Girls in the aisle seats stood up and leaned over those in the window seats, desperate to see the house, but there wasn't a building in sight.

Then they rounded a bend, and the coach erupted into gasps and shrieks of excitement.

*Gosh*, thought Sidney. The house was even grander than she had imagined. Its honey-coloured stone walls glowed golden in the afternoon heat, and the glass glittered in its huge mullioned windows. But the courtyard was full of furniture and packing cases, apart from a path that had been cleared from the terrace to the main entrance.

"Look, all our desks!" said Ginny. "Gosh, I hope they're not going to make us carry them in."

The coach stopped in front of the terrace. From the seat beside the driver, Miss Verney stood up and clapped her hands.

"Silence, girls! Sit down in your seats *at once*!"

Everybody sat down.

13

"When I instruct you to do so, and *not* before, you will file off the coach behind Miss Barnet. Gas masks are to be worn across the body, with the strap on the left shoulder. If you have removed your blazer for the journey, you must put it on when I ask you to – *when* I ask you to and *not* before, Amanda Chesham," she said, with a steely glare at a girl in Sidney's form. "I shall check your appearance as you leave the coach, and I shall expect to see all girls with straight stockings, blazers fully buttoned and hats at the correct angle. First impressions are vitally important, and the good name of St Olave's depends on each and every one of you being properly turned out at all times. It is, of course, imperative that you remain in complete silence from this point until you are in your new dormitories."

Sidney reached up to the luggage rack for her straw boater and gas mask. Trust Miss Verney to do her absolute best to crush the excitement. The rumour was that her fiancé had been killed in the Great War, but it was hard to feel much sympathy when she hid her broken heart beneath endless layers of withering scorn. Miss Verney, Sidney had quickly discovered, was the sort of teacher who had favourites. And Sidney was not one of them.

Fifty pairs of sensible school shoes crunched on the gravel as the girls lined up in silence on the drive, facing the house, hands loosely clasped in front of them in the approved posture. The other coach, with the girls whose surnames came in the second half of the alphabet, rumbled up the drive and stopped on the gravel.

"No turning round, girls," ordered Miss Verney. "Amanda Chesham, stop fidgeting."

Amanda was not a favourite either.

Obediently facing forward, Sidney heard more crunching of gravel and the occasional order from Miss Newsom, the terrifyingly energetic games mistress in charge of the second coach. Amanda turned round to look and was immediately given an order mark.

Feeling very daring, because she wouldn't have been at all surprised to be given an order mark for moving her eyes, Sidney gazed up at the house. A servant girl with bright red hair was looking out of a ground-floor window. She stared at the massed ranks of schoolgirls as though she didn't much like what she saw.

There was a ripple of movement in the lines as Miss Hathersage walked out on to the terrace, a tall, imposing presence in an elegant tweed suit and low-heeled, side-buttoned shoes.

"Ooh, the Sage has new clothes," whispered Lucy Cuthbert, who stood next to Sidney.

Behind Miss Hathersage scuttled her ever-present shadow, Miss Rutter.

"Rutty hasn't," whispered Moira, on Sidney's right. "She's worn that suit every day for two years."

When Sidney looked back at the window, the red-haired servant had gone.

At a nod from Miss Hathersage, Miss Rutter stepped carefully across the courtyard and stood at the top of the steps that led to the drive, her bony hands clasped tightly together. "Welcome to St Olave's at Stanbrook, girls," she said in her reedy voice. "Please follow me to the terrace in a neat and seemly line. When Miss Hathersage has greeted you, you will proceed into the Great Hall, where you will be given your dormitory lists and instructions for the rest of the day."

They processed across the courtyard, gazing at the contents of their classrooms spread out on either side of them.

"Welcome, Sidney," said Miss Hathersage with a firm handshake.

"Thank you, madam," Sidney replied, and she followed Lucy through the front door, across the shiny marble floor of the entrance hall. From a room on the left came thumping and bumping sounds, as though furniture was being moved.

The Great Hall looked far too grand for a school. Life-sized portraits in gilt frames stared disapprovingly from every wall. They were absolutely the type to come alive at night, Sidney thought, already planning her next letter to George.

Miss Hathersage walked to the front. "Please be seated," she said.

There was a cacophony of shuffles, squeaks and thuds as the girls settled themselves cross-legged on the polished floor. As she sat down in the row behind Lucinda, Ginny and Phyllis, Sidney noticed a familiar object on the marble mantelpiece behind the headmistress. It was a varnished wooden board with the school motto printed in gold lettering.

## Her voice was ever soft, gentle and low – an excellent thing in woman.

It was Shakespeare, apparently, and any girl caught shouting or laughing in an unladylike fashion would have to write it out a hundred times. Miss Hathersage prowled the corridors during lessons, and if she heard the faintest hint of a sound from inside a classroom, then the owner of the uncouth voice would be summoned to her study.

The headmistress waited for total silence, and then she said, "Good afternoon, girls." She gave the pupils one of her rare smiles. "We will have our first proper assembly tomorrow morning. You have had a long journey, and I'm sure you are all looking forward to seeing your dormitories in this beautiful house, which has been so graciously lent to us by his lordship, the Earl of Stanbrook."

No wonder she was smiling. She was a terrific snob, and she could rarely have had so much opportunity to pepper her sentences with the name of a peer of the realm.

"Certain areas of the house and grounds are out of bounds to girls, of course," she continued. "These include the stable yard, the library and, naturally, the family's private apartments. We must at all times remember that Stanbrook is a family home. We are extraordinarily privileged to be allowed to share it, and I know you will treat these boundaries with the utmost respect.

"As for the dormitory arrangements, your dormitories here do not have the space for a chest of drawers each, as you have been used to in Sussex. Instead, you will keep your possessions in your trunks, stored under your beds. You each have a chair beside your bed, on which you will keep your washing things. Your uniform is to be laid neatly over the back of your chair at night, and your shoes kept under your chair. There will be an air raid practice after supper, so that you will all know exactly what to do if the siren sounds. Now, when I ask you to stand, please wait for your housemistress to call your name and escort you to your room, where you will change into your indoor shoes and wash before supper."

Sidney's housemistress, Miss Welbeck, stepped forward and put on her glasses. She was dressed in brown, as usual, her hair pulled back in a tight bun. Sidney waited for what seemed like hours as she read out the dormitory lists.

"Finally, in Dormitory Twelve," said Miss Welbeck, "Lucinda Gore-Withers…"

*Oh, please not with her*, Sidney thought.

"Virginia Hamilton," continued the housemistress. "Phyllis Lethbridge. Sidney Dashworth."

Horrors!

She saw Lucinda turn to Ginny and whisper, "Who's Sidney Dashworth?"

"You know, the new girl," whispered Ginny. "In our compartment on the train."

Lucinda looked blank. "It was just us three in the compartment."

"No, she was sitting in the corner. Writing." Ginny glanced back at Sidney with a brief apologetic smile.

"Oh, *her*," said Lucinda, turning and giving Sidney a withering glance that took in every inch of her from her hat to her shoes. "What a dreadful bore."

# CHAPTER THREE

## Absolutely Priceless

As the housemaids heaved the final table into place, a blonde-haired girl a bit older than Nancy walked into the dining room. She wore a similar uniform, except her dress was blue instead of green. Rosa introduced her as Florence, the kitchen maid.

"Hello, Nancy," said Florence. "Welcome to the madhouse."

Nancy liked the look of Florence. She had a round freckled face and a lively, good-humoured expression.

"Did you see the posh girls?" Florence said. "Funny-looking lot, aren't they?"

"I thought it was your afternoon off," Rosa said.

"So did I," said Florence, "but Mr A just cancelled it with not so much as an apology. I tell you, the sooner I get out of here the better. No more bowing and scraping to the idle rich. I'm joining the ATS the moment I'm eighteen."

"I'd like to join the ATS too," said Nancy. She had seen pictures of girls working as mechanics in the Auxiliary Territorial Service, wearing overalls just like the men. "But the war will probably be over before I'm eighteen."

"Looks like it'll be over pretty soon," said Florence. "They say Hitler's boasting he'll have his men in Britain by the end of June."

Nancy felt cold inside. She tried to avoid the news these days. She didn't want to think about what her brother might be going through.

"Bad luck, Nancy, arriving today," said Florence, as they set the chairs round the tables. "I can't believe they got you working without even showing you your room first."

*Her* room! Surely she wouldn't have a room to herself?

"Will I be sharing with you?" Nancy asked.

"No, you'll have your own room," said Florence. She laughed. "You can have three or four if you like. There's barely any live-in servants any more. Everyone who's not too old or too young has gone off to do war work. There's a Spitfire factory nearby; it pays better and the hours are more regular."

"Gosh, my own room!" said Nancy. She had never even had a bed to herself, let alone a room. She had always shared with her younger sisters.

"And there's a servants' bathroom at the end of the corridor," said Florence. "With a bath and a basin, as well as a lavatory, all with running water. The last earl had it installed, God rest his soul."

"Crikey," said Nancy. "An indoor lavatory *and* my own room!"

"It might seem like a luxury now," said Florence,

"but when winter comes you'll wish you were sharing a bed. It's so cold you'll need to sleep in every stitch of clothing you own. And it's not just our attics either. The family's rooms are freezing, even with the fires. Isn't that right, Rosa?"

"I have never known such cold," said Rosa, setting a chair down with a shudder.

"Really?" said Nancy, astonished. "Even in Austria?"

"Well, look at it," said Florence, before Rosa had a chance to reply. "A couple of fires are never going to warm rooms the size of these. But you know what?" she said, as she set out chairs with impressive speed. "Albert showed me round the greenhouses one day, and, no word of a lie, there's a special furnace and a whole network of heating pipes in there. So here's one of the richest men in the country, with his house so cold we're all in danger of pneumonia, but there's underfloor heating for his pineapples. If that isn't full-blown lunacy, you tell me what is."

"Do you see the earl much?" Nancy asked, with a little lurch in her stomach as she remembered the disturbing conversation she'd overheard.

Florence shook her head. "His lordship talks to Mr Armitage. And the dowager duchess – that's his lordship's mother – has her lady's maid. But the rest of us barely see them. As far as his lordship's concerned, the female servants are invisible. The house stays clean all by itself, and his meals are made by magic."

Rosa raised her eyebrows. "Not only earls. Many

men in my family think the same."

When they had set out all the chairs, Mr Armitage told them to bring the crates full of books into the Great Hall.

"Funny how he stands around directing everybody, and we do all the work," muttered Florence.

The last of the schoolgirls were filing up the stairs to their dormitories as the maids walked through the hall. From the front steps, Nancy saw a procession of grey vans approaching the house.

"That must be his lordship's art," said Rosa.

"All those vans?" said Nancy. "He must have more art than the National Gallery."

"His lordship collects antique Chinese porcelain. He has one of the greatest collections in the world."

Nancy marvelled at Rosa's English. Imagine knowing how to say "antique Chinese porcelain" in another language!

She picked up a crate, and a heap of exercise books slithered across the top. Nancy read the names. Lucy Cuthbert. Lucinda Gore-Withers. Sidney Dashworth.

*Lucky little rich girls*, she thought. And they probably didn't even appreciate it. Why did they need a good education, when they would never have to earn their own living?

Lugging the crate into the entrance hall, she was surprised to see a tiny beautiful old lady walking slowly down the stairs. She wore an exquisite pale blue silk dress with matching shoes, and she leaned on the arm of a serious-looking woman in a brown-wool dress buttoned up to the chin.

The old lady looked at Nancy and gave a delighted gasp. "Margaret!" she exclaimed.

Nancy glanced behind her, but there was nobody there.

"That's not Margaret, my lady," said the other woman, looking at Nancy's uniform. "I assume you are the new housemaid?"

"Yes, ma'am," Nancy replied. "I'm Nancy."

The old lady didn't seem to hear. As they reached the bottom of the stairs, she touched Nancy's hair with trembling hands. Nancy was shocked at how thin and frail her fingers were. Her skin looked almost transparent.

"Come and have tea with me, Margaret. We have so much to talk about. Hilda, order extra tea for Margaret, please. And raspberry jam."

She gave Nancy a smile of pure love. Nancy had never felt so awkward in her life. Mum had always said aristocrats were eccentric, but she hadn't thought they'd be as odd as this.

"That's not Margaret, my lady," Hilda repeated. "She's got similar red hair, but she's not—"

She suddenly stopped and bobbed a curtsy. Nancy turned and saw Lord Evesham walking into the entrance hall. She took a few steps back, hoping to make herself invisible.

A strange fearful look came over the old lady's face as she saw the earl. "Gerald!" she said. "Are you in trouble again?"

He gave a little laugh. "What are you talking

about, Mother? Of course I'm not in trouble."

Mother? So the old lady must be the Dowager Countess of Stanbrook. No wonder she was so beautifully dressed.

Lord Evesham was about to say something else when two removal men came into the hall, buckling under the weight of a long sausage-shaped bundle. Lord Evesham leaped towards them, clapping his hands to his head in horror. "Great Scott, don't manhandle it like a dead pig!" he exclaimed through clenched teeth. "It's an extremely delicate Flemish tapestry. You're risking permanent damage to the stitching."

"Yes, sir," the men mumbled. "Sorry, sir."

"Careful!" he shrieked, as they turned into the corridor. "You could have knocked the painting off the wall. Armitage, you're supposed to be supervising these halfwits! Oh, get out of the way, man!" he said, shooing the butler away. "I can see I'll have to do everything myself, as usual."

*Wow*, thought Nancy. *What a fusspot.*

She carried her crate into the Great Hall, which was even bigger than the dining room. Albert was setting down a crate at the far end.

He winked at Nancy on his way out. "All right, carrot top?"

Nancy rolled her eyes, but she didn't really mind. He seemed friendly enough.

Miss Rutter, the deputy headmistress, hurried towards Nancy, clutching the classroom lists. She looked like a smaller, dustier version of

Miss Hathersage.

She inspected the label on the side of the crate. "Lower Fourth," she said in a slightly breathless voice. "Over there, underneath the portrait of the third earl."

"Yes, ma'am," said Nancy.

As she returned to the entrance hall, the dowager said, "Margaret, you will come for tea, won't you? I have so much to tell you."

Nancy smiled awkwardly and glanced at Hilda, who said, "Shall we go through to the library, my lady?"

Lord Evesham stood at the front door, directing the stream of removal men. As Nancy walked past, he stopped a nervous-looking boy who was cradling a box as tenderly as though it were a newborn infant. "Those vases are absolutely priceless," he said. "Be *extremely* careful on the stairs. *Extremely* careful, do you understand?"

Nancy read the label on the box.

### Ming Dynasty
AD 1372

Almost six hundred years old! No wonder he wanted them safely out of London before Hitler got to them.

As she and Florence carried more crates up the steps, the earl summoned Mr Armitage to him.

"Why are the statues in the Long Gallery not protected by dust sheets, Armitage?"

"There is rather a shortage of fabric these days, my lord. It has been difficult to obtain sufficient to black out the entire house, and the blackout had to be our priority."

"Good grief, the fuss everybody makes about the blackout! Hang the blackout! It's the art that matters, Armitage. If a stray bomb were to fall here, the statues could suffer terrible damage from flying glass. See that they're covered."

"Yes, sir."

"That's typical, that is," Florence muttered. "It's all very well for him not to worry about the blackout. He knows he'd never be prosecuted."

"Does he?" said Nancy. "Why?"

"Because the rich never are. Some poor widow leaves a tiny gleam of light between her blinds and she'll be up before the magistrate, but Lord Evesham could have every light in the house blazing and nobody would dare lift a finger against him. There's one law for the rich and one for the poor, Nancy, and don't you ever forget it."

# CHAPTER FOUR

## An Earl, an Order Mark and a Housemaid

There were four beds in the dormitory: three in a row facing into the room, and one placed sideways under the window. Lucinda scanned the room and flung her overnight bag on the bed in the corner by the fireplace.

"You take that one," she ordered Ginny. Ginny dropped her bag on the bed next to Lucinda's, and Phyllis, after a nervous glance at Sidney, put hers on the bed next to Ginny's.

*Good*, Sidney thought. Far better to be on her own than cramped up with that lot. Besides, the window had a view over the stable block and gardens, and, beyond them, across woods and meadows with little towns and villages dotted among them, right to the hazy blue hills in the distance. She set her overnight bag on the bed and started unpacking.

Ginny took out her royal family scrapbook and slipped it under her pillow. "Do you think this house is haunted?" she said. "I swear those portraits were following me with their eyes. I bet they come alive at night."

Sidney felt a new respect for Ginny, but Lucinda gave a little shudder before shooting her a scornful look. "Don't be ridiculous. Move that bag off the bed, new girl."

She elbowed Sidney out of the way, kneeled on her bed and flung up the sash as if she owned the place. Gazing across the gardens, she said, "I wonder if Lord Evesham is here or in his London house."

"Do you know Lord Evesham?" asked Ginny.

"Not exactly," said Lucinda, making herself at home on Sidney's bed. "But my father told me all about him. You must have heard of him; he's a war hero. He was a pilot in the Great War, a flying ace. He won medals. He's been flying planes ever since, and he's made record-breaking non-stop flights between London and Oslo *and* between London and Berlin. He works for the Air Ministry now, so I expect he's in London a lot, but he must be here sometimes."

"How exciting!" said Phyllis, placing a framed photograph of a horse and a dog on her chair. Each girl was allowed to display one photograph. "Have you seen a picture of him? Is he handsome? Is he married?"

"He must be quite old if he fought in the last war," said Ginny.

"He's not that old," said Lucinda. "Around forty, I think. And he was married, but his wife died last year. It must be hard for him to manage all his houses and estates without a wife. He has a castle in Ireland too, you know, and all sorts of other places."

So Lucinda was planning to become a countess. Of course she was.

"Oh!" Lucinda squealed. "There he is!"

Ginny and Phyllis gasped and scrambled on to the bed on either side of her.

"Stop jostling, Phyllis," said Lucinda. "Give me some space."

Phyllis edged away, looking crestfallen. Sidney stood behind them, where she had a good view over their heads. She didn't want to seem interested in anything Lucinda was interested in, but she was curious to see what Lord Evesham looked like.

A man on a gleaming chestnut horse came into the stable yard. There was something about the shape of his face that meant he could have been dressed in rags and you'd still have known he was an aristocrat.

"Oh, what a *beautiful* hunter," said Phyllis.

"Honestly, Phyllis, do you think about nothing but horses?" said Lucinda. "Horrible smelly, snorting beasts."

The man dismounted and handed the reins to a boy who had appeared from a stable.

"He's very handsome," said Lucinda.

"The stable boy?" said Ginny.

"No, idiot, Lord Evesham, obviously."

"I prefer the stable boy," said Ginny.

"Well, you're welcome to him. I'd have thought—"

She broke off as the door opened. They turned to see Miss Welbeck glowering in the doorway.

"Lucinda, Virginia, Phyllis, off the bed at *once*! You should be ashamed of yourselves. Do your mothers allow you to kneel on your beds wearing outdoor shoes? Order marks for all three of you.

Change into your indoor shoes, unpack your night things and join the queue for the washbasins. And make sure you all come down to supper together. No girl is to wander about the house alone."

She left the room and they clambered off the bed. Lucinda was red-faced with suppressed rage. Phyllis looked close to tears.

"I can't believe we've got order marks already," muttered Ginny.

Order marks cancelled out house points, so girls who accumulated them could become very unpopular.

In silence they changed their shoes and unpacked. Sidney took out her framed photograph of George in his uniform and placed it on her chair.

"Gosh, is that your brother?" asked Ginny. "He's awfully handsome."

Sidney felt a warm glow of pride.

"Is he in the RAF?" asked Phyllis.

"Yes, he flies a Spitfire," said Sidney, trying to sound like that wasn't anything to boast about.

"He must be terribly brave," said Ginny.

Lucinda shot Sidney a poisonous look. Her photograph showed a glamorous-looking couple, presumably her parents, standing outside a vast house surrounded by uniformed Indian servants. "Will you hurry up?" she said. "Or do you want to get us all another order mark?"

St Olave's girls were not allowed to run, except in an elegant manner on the tennis or netball court. But as soon as the Dormitory Twelve girls had given their hands a quick wash, they sprinted down the back stairs, confident that all the mistresses would already be in the dining hall. The main staircase, of course, was out of bounds.

At a turn in the staircase, Lucinda almost bumped into two maids walking up, carrying armfuls of black fabric. Sidney recognised one of them as the red-haired girl who'd been looking out of the dining-room window earlier.

Lucinda shoved past the dark-haired maid, who stumbled and fell into the other girl. They grabbed the banister rail to steady themselves, and some of the fabric fell to the floor.

"Steady on," the red-haired girl said to Lucinda. "You nearly pushed us down the stairs."

Lucinda raised her eyebrows and gave them her haughtiest look. "Perhaps you should use the stairs at a more convenient time."

The dark-haired girl kept her eyes on the ground, but the red-haired one gave Lucinda an evil stare as she bent to pick up the fallen fabric.

Lucinda kicked aside a sheet in her way. "I can't believe they still haven't arranged the blackout," she said as she ran on down the stairs, followed by Ginny and Phyllis. "It's a disgrace. So badly organised, when they've had absolute weeks to prepare. My father would have had them dismissed for that."

Sidney was at the back of the group. As she clattered down the stairs, she heard the red-haired girl say, "What did I tell you? Spoilt little snobs, every one of them."

# CHAPTER FIVE

# The Lady in Grey

"Are you sure the dining room's this way?" asked Ginny, as Lucinda led them along the ground-floor corridor.

"Of course it is," said Lucinda. "Hurry up, will you?"

Even Lucinda didn't dare run along the corridor, but every St Olave's girl had perfected the art of fast walking. So when a tiny old lady emerged silently from a doorway, Lucinda almost mowed her down.

"Oh, my goodness, I'm so terribly sorry, ma'am," she gasped, hastily stepping back.

The lady was exquisitely dressed in pale blue silk, with beautifully waved white hair and three strings of pearls round her neck. Lucinda had obviously realised that here was somebody worth being polite to.

"Come in, come in," said the lady in a voice that was as soft, gentle and low as Miss Hathersage could have wished. "I'm so glad you came. The spirits are very close now. I can feel their presence."

The girls stared in a highly unladylike way. Lucinda

looked terrified.

"Come into the library, my dears," said the lady, taking Lucinda's arm. "Perhaps the spirits will reveal themselves to you too."

Sidney couldn't believe her luck. So there *were* ghosts here! *And* an eccentric old lady who communicated with them. She couldn't wait to tell George.

The supper bell rang in the distance. Phyllis glanced anxiously at Lucinda.

"Oh, that's terribly kind of you," said Ginny, "but unfortunately we have to go to supper."

The lady took no notice. She had a dreamy look on her face, as though she was living in another world. She ushered them into the library, straight past the sign on the door in Miss Hathersage's handwriting: STRICTLY OUT OF BOUNDS TO PUPILS. Sidney felt a thrill of anticipation.

The library was a high-ceilinged wood-panelled room. An enormous dining table took up most of the floor space. Shelves of leather-bound books lined the walls. A spiral staircase in the far corner led up to a book-lined balcony that ran the whole way round the room.

The girls waited behind the old lady, who closed her eyes and raised her trembling palms upwards. She appeared to be listening for something. After a long silence, in which Sidney hardly dared breathe, she slowly lowered her arms, opened her eyes and turned to them with a wistful smile.

"I am sorry to disappoint you, my dears. Her

presence is no longer with us."

They stood still, waiting for her to continue, but she closed her eyes again and remained silent.

Eventually Sidney's curiosity overcame her respect. "May I ask, ma'am, whose presence?"

The old lady opened her eyes. "Why, the Lady in Grey."

Sidney's eyes widened. How perfectly thrilling!

They waited for more, but the lady stayed silent.

"May I ask who the Lady in Grey is?" asked Sidney.

The lady laughed affectionately. "Why, girls, I've told you her story so many times."

Ginny and Lucinda exchanged glances. Desperate that they shouldn't break the illusion, Sidney asked, "Could you tell us again?"

The lady's clouded eyes became more animated. "The Lady in Grey," she began, as though repeating words she knew by heart, "was the wife of the second earl, hundreds of years ago. He was in his forties when he married her, and she was a girl of only fifteen."

Ginny gave Lucinda a meaningful look. Lucinda pretended not to see it.

"He married her for her fortune, but she was deeply in love with him. She was young and innocent, and she had no idea that he was in love with another woman. From the moment they were married, he was cruel and neglectful. He spent almost all his time away from Stanbrook, never telling her when or why he was going. He was away so much that she grew mad with loneliness."

Her eyes clouded again and lost their focus. She looked around the room, as if trying to remind herself where she was. She took a couple of halting steps towards the door.

"What happened next?" asked Sidney, longing to hear the rest of the story. "After she grew mad with loneliness?"

The lady seemed to make a big effort to focus. Her eyes found Sidney's, and she frowned in concentration.

"Mad with loneliness," she murmured. "Mad with loneliness. Pacing the house, up and down, up and down, night after night, ever more frantic."

She paused, and her voice quietened. "One night, she failed to return from her moonlit wanderings. Her maid entered her room the following morning and discovered that the bed hadn't been slept in. The servants were called to search the grounds, and her poor maid..."

Her voice lowered to a whisper. "Her poor maid found her body, lying on the lawn, fallen from the roof. Nobody knows whether it was suicide or a terrible accident, but ever since then, there have been reports of a Lady in Grey wandering the house and gardens of Stanbrook at night."

She stopped. The girls stood, frozen. Lucinda had turned white with terror.

"Have you ever seen her?" Sidney asked, thrilled to the core. But the lady's eyes had clouded again.

Suddenly the door was wrenched open. The girls

all jumped, and Lucinda shrieked. They spun round to see Miss Welbeck glaring from the doorway.

"You four again! Late for supper and in a room that is strictly out of bounds. Five order marks for each of you, and report to the headmistress's study immediately after supper. Not that there will be any— Oh, I'm terribly sorry, your ladyship. I do beg your pardon."

Ginny had stepped back to reveal the old lady, shrinking in fear from Miss Welbeck's harsh voice.

Miss Welbeck blushed and bobbed a clumsy sort of curtsy. But the old lady was looking past the teacher, towards the doorway. She gave a beaming smile, as though she had recognised a long-lost friend.

"Margaret! Dear Margaret."

Sidney turned and saw that she seemed to be greeting the red-haired maid, who was walking along the corridor with the other maid. How odd.

The girl gave an awkward smile and bobbed a little curtsy. The dark-haired maid gave her a curious look.

So the red-haired maid was called Margaret. And the lady seemed fond of her, for some reason. How extraordinary. She was obviously as batty as an attic, poor dear.

As the maids continued on their way, a woman in a brown suit appeared in the doorway and sighed with relief.

"Oh, there you are, my lady. Where have you been? I've been searching everywhere for you."

It turned out that the old lady was actually the dowager countess, the earl's mother, and the other woman was her lady's maid, Miss Morris. The maid explained to Miss Welbeck that the dowager was "a little confused" but had obviously taken a liking to the girls. After that, Miss Welbeck couldn't very well punish them, so they were allowed to take their places at table and make conversation during supper.

In Sussex they had taken meals in their houses, so it was strange to eat with the entire school. Even stranger was seeing their plain school tables and chairs transplanted to this enormous grand dining room.

"Why have they turned all the pictures back to front?" asked Phyllis, gazing at the blank canvas backs of the huge paintings.

"Perhaps they thought we'd draw moustaches on the portraits," said Mary.

Jean, the prefect at the head of their table, smiled. "Perhaps they didn't want the ancient earls to be forced to watch us eating potato pie."

"I bet they never had rationing," said Ginny, poking a fork beneath the potato pastry to reveal the potato filling. "I bet they feasted on lobster and ice cream every day."

When everybody had been served, Lucinda turned to Sidney and asked, "Would you like some salt?"

"No, thank you," she replied. "Would you?"

"Yes, please," Lucinda said coldly.

It was one of many mealtime rules at St Olave's that you were not allowed to ask for anything for yourself. So if you wanted the salt, you had to ask the girl sitting nearest the salt whether she would like some, and then she would ask you whether you would like some in turn. All these things were supposed to teach selflessness and good manners, but actually they just meant everybody's food was cold before they started.

"Did you know we can choose German or Latin next year?" said Amanda. "I'm going to do German. If we lose the war, it will come in handy."

"Don't talk like that," said Ginny. "Of course we'll win the war."

"I don't see how we can," said Amanda. "France will have to surrender soon, and then the Germans will cross the Channel."

"They won't dare," said Mary. "My father says our navy is the best in the world."

"Oh, well, if your father says so…" said Lucinda sarcastically.

"Anyway, if they do come over here, we'll defeat them," said Ginny.

"How?" said Amanda. "Britain can't possibly defeat Germany alone. Hitler will destroy the RAF and bomb all our ships, and then he'll send in planeloads of parachutists with machine guns before he ships over the rest of his men. And our soldiers are all trapped on the French coast. Do you really think a jumble of old men and farmhands in the Local Defence Volunteers, with their pitchforks and air rifles, have any chance of stopping the Nazis? No, I'd choose German if I were you, girls, and start practising your Hitler salutes. We haven't got a hope."

# George to Sidney

Dear little sis,

We've just got a gramophone in the mess, and it makes things a sight more jolly, I must say. We've a few good jazz records and we're going to club together to get some more. I get a fair bit of reading done too. I've just finished *Three Men in a Boat* – funniest thing I've ever read. I'll send it on to you if it won't get you expelled for being in possession of more than one book. Never heard such an idiotic rule in my life. You could send *The Murder of Roger Ackroyd* in exchange once you've finished it if you like. We're always in need of more reading material, what with all the hanging around, and the chaps like detective stories. I've asked the parents to send more too.

I must say, the food's jolly good here – eggs and bacon every day for breakfast if we want it – a sight better than the lumpy porridge you poor females are force-fed. Sounds worse than the army in that school of yours, and army rations are frightful from what we hear – the army chaps are awfully jealous of us. You should really lead the troops out on a general strike.

I've been thinking I'd like to take up farming once this is all over. Do you remember the summer we went to Devon, and all those picnics we had, with birds and butterflies and wildflowers everywhere, and swimming in the river with the seal popping up and swimming alongside us? Remember the cress we grew on the windowsill and made into egg and cress sandwiches – I can taste them now. After the war I'm planning to rent a little farm down there – just a small place at first, but I shall make a go of it. You can come for holidays – working holidays, mind you – bring a few of your schoolfriends if they don't mind mucking out pigs.

Do you remember when we found the butterfly chrysalis on a twig, and we kept it in a big jar? And one morning we came downstairs to find a peacock butterfly hatching out, and we took the jar into the garden, and the butterfly flew away. Do you remember how sorry we felt for it, thinking butterflies only lived for a day? Well, I just found out from a chap here who's frightfully knowledgeable about such things, that peacock butterflies actually hibernate in autumn and emerge again in spring. Isn't that a cheering thought? And he said those circles on their wing tips that look like huge eyes are there to imitate a much bigger, more aggressive animal to frighten predators away. Pretty clever of them, eh? If they manage to dodge the predators, they live about eleven months, apparently. Not a long life, but a lot longer than we imagined our butterfly would have.

Must go now. Eagerly awaiting your next bulletin. Be good – and if you can't be good, don't get caught.

Your loving brother

# CHAPTER SIX

## A Shock in
## the Night

Sometime on Saturday night, Sidney awoke with a jolt, her heart pounding. What was that? It had sounded like an explosion. Had it been a dream?

*BANG!* This time the noise was deafening.

"Bombs!" shrieked Ginny, leaping out of bed. "Quick, to the shelter!"

Sidney yanked the curtains open, her heart pounding, and gasped. "Fire!"

"What?" squeaked Phyllis, as she and Ginny scrambled on to Sidney's bed. It was a warm moonlit night, and somewhere in the distant countryside something large was on fire. Vast black plumes of smoke billowed upwards, and the sky was filled with a red glow.

"Quick, to the cellars!" cried Ginny, tugging at Phyllis's nightdress.

Lucinda turned over in bed. "The siren hasn't sounded," she mumbled. "It can't be an air raid. Go back to bed and let me sleep."

"But there was an explosion," said Ginny, "and there's a huge fire. It must have been a bomb."

43

There was a babble of voices, as doors opened all along the corridor. The door to Dormitory Twelve opened and Mary poked her head in.

"Are you going to the shelter?" she asked. "Did you hear the siren?"

Ginny was about to reply when Miss Welbeck appeared behind Mary.

"Girls, go back to bed, please," she said. "The sirens have not sounded. Remember what you were told in your air raid practice. *If* the siren sounds, follow the correct procedure. Now go back to bed in silence."

"Told you," murmured Lucinda, once Miss Welbeck had closed the door. "Stop panicking like cowards and let me sleep. Close the curtains, new girl."

She turned to the wall and pulled the sheet over her head. Ginny made a face behind her back.

As Sidney went to close the curtains, she saw that the red glow in the sky had deepened. But there had been no sound of planes or guns, so it must just be a fire. Those explosions had been enormous, though. Would an ordinary fire cause explosions like that?

On Sunday morning, Amanda hurried into the dining hall for breakfast at the very last minute. She was slightly out of breath and had an air of suppressed excitement about her. She slipped into her seat just as Miss Rutter stood up to say grace.

As soon as Breakfast Notices were over and the girls were allowed to speak, Amanda said, "Guess what? That fire last night was at a Spitfire factory."

Sidney's legs felt wobbly. So it *had* been a bomb then. Of course the Germans would want to destroy a Spitfire factory.

"How do you know?" asked Ginny.

"I went out to the gardens before breakfast, and I asked this boy who works here. He said everyone in the village knows because the auxiliary firemen were called out to help."

"So the factory's close to Stanbrook?" asked Phyllis.

"A few miles away, I think. And guess what?"

"What?" asked Ginny.

Everyone leaned in closer, except for Lucinda, who pretended not to be interested.

In a hushed tone Amanda said, "No German bombers flew over here last night."

"We knew that already," said Lucinda scornfully. "The sirens didn't go off. A factory accident is hardly big news, Amanda."

"That's the thing," said Amanda triumphantly. "It *wasn't* an accident."

There were puzzled looks round the table.

"But if it wasn't a bomb, and it wasn't an accident...?" said Phyllis.

Mary's eyes widened. "You mean somebody started it on purpose?"

"Well, the explosions were enormous, and they completely destroyed the boilers and the generator, which means the factory has no power, so they can't make any Spitfires. And it just makes sense,

45

doesn't it?"

"What does?" asked Phyllis.

"Well, the Germans want to stop us making fighter planes obviously. The more we have, the more likely we are to beat them."

"But you just said there were no German bombers last night," said Sidney, irritation rising inside her. She wished Amanda would stop speaking in riddles.

"That's right," said Amanda. "The factory wasn't destroyed from the air."

Mary gasped. "So it was sabotage?"

"Oh, my goodness!" said Ginny. "Enemy agents right here among us."

"You mean German spies?" asked Phyllis.

Jean frowned. "We shouldn't be spreading rumours. We don't actually know anything."

Nobody took any notice.

"That's exactly what the Local Defence Volunteers are looking out for," said Ginny. "My father's joined, and they're being trained to keep watch for spies and fifth columnists."

"What's a fifth columnist?" asked Phyllis.

Jean jumped in before Lucinda could unleash the full force of her scorn on Phyllis. "They're British people who are secretly working for the Nazis and want Hitler to win the war."

Sidney frowned. "I don't believe fifth columnists really exist. It's just the newspapers being hysterical. No British person would want Hitler to win the war."

Jean shrugged. "Some British people agree with

what he's doing. Like Oswald Mosley and the Blackshirts. They think Hitler's improved Germany by being a strong leader, and they want a fascist government here too."

"No British person would blow up a Spitfire plant," said Mary. "It must have been a German spy."

"That's why the government's rounding up enemy aliens and putting them in internment camps, isn't it?" said Amanda. "To catch all the German spies."

"Let's hope it was a German then," said Ginny. "At least they're easy to spot. If it was a British person secretly working for the Nazis, they might be a lot more difficult to catch."

# CHAPTER SEVEN

## A Secret Passage

In the hour between church and Sunday lunch, the St Olave's girls wrote letters home. Sidney scribbled a brief, dull letter to her parents, and then settled down to write to George, trying not to think too deeply about what he might be doing at that moment.

The girls had no wireless or newspapers, so they didn't hear much war news, but Miss Hathersage had told them the British army was being brought back from Dunkirk on the French coast, where they had been trapped by the Germans. Hundreds of small fishing boats and pleasure boats were heading to France to help rescue the stranded soldiers, but they were being constantly attacked from the air.

Sidney had turned cold when Miss Hathersage said the RAF were fighting off the German bombers. During the prayers in church, she had just repeated in her head, over and over again, *Please, please let George be safe.*

The teachers inspected the girls' letters to check for unsuitable content, so Sidney hid George's letter in her pocket while she showed Miss Welbeck what she'd written to her parents. When Miss Welbeck turned her attention to Mary, Sidney slipped George's letter underneath and dropped them both in the post tray.

Stanbrook House
Sunday 2nd June

Dear Dordy,

Such a thrill to hear about all the little ships crossing the Channel. Are you swooping about in your plane, fighting off the enemy? Do tell, or are you not allowed because of the censors? I'm sure you're being terribly brave and dare-devilish.

This house is simply enorm, hundreds and hundreds of rooms, we barely use half of them – the earl and dowager countess still live in the West Wing. The dowager's divine, you'd simply adore her. She wears the most heavenly clothes and she's completely batty, poor old dear – she talks to the ghosts that supposedly haunt the house, it's so thrilling. Lucinda's terrified of the ghosts, it's so hilare. I don't believe in ghosts – do you?

The gardens are heaven, though so far I've only seen glimpses of them when we're being herded about to ghastly drilling classes. Lucinda is set on marrying the earl, absolutely typical. I pray I'll be there to see it when he completely cuts her dead, what joy. There's a fiery red-haired servant girl who's taken an absolute hate against us, it's extremely amusing.

If you think I'm doing nothing to contribute to the war effort while you're being so heroic, then you're very much

49

mistaken. This afternoon I shall be planting radishes, which, according to Miss Hathersage, is guaranteed to bring us certain victory.

"Why do you call him Dordy?" asked Ginny.

"Ginny! It's beastly form to snoop at other people's letters."

Ginny shrugged and repeated the question.

"Apparently when I was little that was the closest I could get to pronouncing his name," said Sidney. "And it sort of stuck. I don't call him that to his face any more, only in letters."

"You are lucky to have an older brother. Younger brothers are beastly. Does he bring his RAF friends home?"

"Sometimes," said Sidney, thinking of Anthony, the handsome fighter pilot with the dreamy smile who had come home with George on his last leave.

"How heavenly," said Ginny. "Do they wear their uniforms? The RAF uniform is so much nicer than the army's."

Lucinda leaned forward. "From what I've heard," she said, "the Air Force does nothing except preen in their uniforms. The army and the navy are doing all the real fighting."

"If the RAF are doing nothing, that doesn't reflect very well on Lord Evesham, does it?" Sidney replied. "Considering he's so high up in the Air Ministry."

Lucinda glowered. She seemed to be trying to come up with a retort, but she clearly couldn't think of one, so she tossed her head and went back to her letter. It was a delightful moment.

Sunday afternoons at St Olave's were for war work. In Sussex, this had meant knitting or sewing comforts for the troops, but now the girls were given the option of digging for victory instead. Sidney had chosen to dig. Not that she was planning to do any actual digging, obviously, but presumably that was just a figure of speech. And anything would be preferable to sewing or knitting, both deathly forms of torture. Her one half-hearted attempt at a sock had not been a success.

"Gracious," Pamela, the duty prefect, had said, inspecting its unorthodox shape. "Are you knitting for a troll?"

"Oh, are there trolls here?" Sidney had replied. "How perfectly sweet. I'd *love* to knit for a troll."

Pamela had given her an order mark for insolence, and Sidney had related the story gleefully in her letter to George.

Miss Newsom bustled the gardening volunteers across the lawns and through a door into the huge walled kitchen garden.

"Isn't this fun!" she said. "Aren't we lucky, girls!"

The garden was on a south-facing slope, and beyond the wall at the bottom was an ornamental lake surrounded by willow trees. On the far side of the lake, the meadows were dotted with grazing sheep and lambs. It was all divinely pretty.

A stern-looking man in a leather apron walked over to meet them. He introduced himself as Mr

Atkins, the head gardener. He looked as though he hadn't smiled since Queen Victoria was on the throne.

"Any of you done any gardening before?" he asked.

Sidney raised her hand, which was an utter lie. All she'd ever done was cut a few sweet peas and roses for the house, but she hoped she'd be given a more interesting job if Mr Atkins thought she was an expert gardener.

He showed them the beds that had been prepared. The girls who hadn't gardened before had to work under his supervision, but he sent Sidney over to a bed by the wall on her own.

"Sowing salad crops," he said. "Follow the instructions on the packets."

The soil in the bed had recently been dug over. A square of oilcloth for kneeling on lay on the grass. Beside it was a box containing a fork and trowel, wooden labels, a stubby pencil and several packets of seeds.

Sidney picked up a pack of lettuce seeds, glanced over the instructions and started making patterns in the soil with her trowel.

A boy with curly brown hair springing out from his cap was pruning the fruit trees trained against the wall. He only had one arm; his other sleeve was tucked into his jacket pocket.

"Hello," he said. "You one of the schoolgirls?"

"No," said Sidney. "I'm a secret agent, sent down from the Ministry."

"Course you are. What you looking for?"

"Enemy agents disguised as gardeners."

He laughed and jerked his thumb towards Mr Atkins. "I'd keep an eye on him then, if I was you."

Sidney raised her eyebrows. "If you think you're going to put me off the scent that easily, you're very much mistaken. I'm a trained professional."

He shrugged and crouched down to pull off the suckers at the base of the fruit tree. "You must know all about the secret passage then, seeing as you're a secret agent and all."

Sidney stared at him, her heartbeat speeding up. A secret passage? Was he serious?

She tried not to look too interested. "Certainly I do."

He nodded. "Thought you would."

Infuriatingly he turned away from her and continued to work in silence. Sidney waited for him to crack. She was so absorbed in the idea of the secret passage that she didn't notice Mr Atkins approaching.

"What the heck do you think you're playing at?" he said, scowling at the curving patterns in the soil.

"Digging trenches, sir, as you asked me to," said Sidney, adopting a wounded tone.

"They're weaving about all over the place."

"Is that wrong, sir?"

"Of course it's wrong! Trenches is straight lines."

"Oh, gosh, I'm most awfully sorry. I thought they'd look pretty like this."

He made a sound of utter disgust. "Start again in straight lines. And get a blessed move on."

He stomped off, muttering furious oaths about useless schoolgirls, which Sidney stored up to write to George. She was tempted to sow her lettuces in the shape of a rude word, which would be terrific fun once the seeds sprouted, at least for a few minutes before she was expelled. But Mr Atkins was keeping his beady eye on her, and the thought of being taken off gardening and sent to knit ghastly khaki balaclavas in the depressing presence of Miss Rutter was enough to make her draw her trowel through the soil in a line that was more or less straight.

That teasing gardener's boy was working his way down the wall away from her. How annoying; she was going to have to swallow her pride.

She cleared her throat. "About that secret passage. I need to ask you, in my official capacity, exactly what you know about it."

He grinned triumphantly. "Knew you'd ask me sooner or later."

Sidney gave him a haughty look. "I hope I don't need to remind you that, as an employee of His Majesty's Government, I am legally entitled to compel you to answer."

"Go on then. Show me your papers."

This could clearly go on forever, and Sidney could see Mr Atkins scowling in their direction.

"Just tell me about the secret passage. Please?"

The boy looked satisfied. "My grandad told me about it. He was head gardener here before the

Great War. Twenty full-time gardeners under him in them days."

He paused, evidently hoping that Sidney would be impressed.

"Go on," she said. "What did he tell you?"

He shrugged, clearly annoyed at her lack of reaction. "Just that there's a secret passage what leads to the strong room, and it was used by smugglers in the old days. But my dad says it's all rubbish. His lordship stores the family treasures in the strong room, and my dad says he wouldn't do that if somebody could get to it through a secret passage." He turned back to his work.

"And where is the strong room?" asked Sidney.

The boy raised his eyebrows. "Thinking of stealing the silver, are you? How would I know where it is? I'm just the gardener's boy."

Miss Newsom, bustling about checking everybody's work, hurried towards Sidney with an encouraging smile.

"No time for chitter-chatter, Sidney!" she chirruped. "Remember you're serving your country."

"Yes, madam." Sidney sprinkled soil over the seeds. She waited for the teacher to move away, but Miss Newsom hovered close by, making uplifting remarks to a couple of fifth-formers.

Unable to ask more questions, Sidney started thinking. Did this boy's grandad really know about a secret passage, or was it just a myth? Sidney had read enough detective stories to know that the entrance to a secret passage might be hidden behind a painting, or a panelled wall, or a door disguised as a bookcase, or even a trapdoor concealed beneath a carpet. It would take months to search a house the size of Stanbrook. But imagine how thrilling it would be to find it!

# CHAPTER EIGHT

# A Midnight Meeting

At five o'clock the girls were sent indoors to wash and change for supper. Sidney made sure she was at the back of the group. She planned to slip unnoticed into the out-of-bounds library as they passed it. With its panelled walls lined with bookcases, it was the perfect place for the entrance to a secret passage. She reckoned she could spend twenty minutes searching and still have time to run upstairs and change. Lucinda wouldn't notice whether she was there or not, and she trusted Phyllis and Ginny not to snitch. They might hang around with Lucinda, but she was pretty sure they weren't sneaks.

Miss Newsom led them across the lawn, enthusing about the marvellous war work they had done. Loitering behind the others, Sidney glimpsed Lord Evesham and a woman strolling along a path on the other side of the rose garden, deep in conversation. The woman had beautifully waved blonde shoulder-length hair and wore an elegant emerald-green dress.

Was she his girlfriend? Imagine if he was about to

propose! What a thrill that would be, and what an utter blow for Lucinda.

As Miss Newsom led the crocodile of girls into the house, Sidney slipped through the open gateway into the rose garden. She walked across it and out of the gateway on the other side. Lord Evesham and the woman were a few yards ahead of her. If they glanced back, she would pretend to be admiring the flowers in the herbaceous borders.

She followed them at a distance, feeling thrillingly detective-ish. She was already planning how she would report her adventure to George.

"You haven't told anybody except Lonsdale?" Lord Evesham said in a low voice.

"Not a soul."

"Good. Once the date is set, things will change, of course, but it's best to keep it between us for the present."

The woman nodded.

*Once the date is set...*

Could it be a wedding date? How thrilling if they were secretly engaged! And what a joy it would be to report it to Lucinda.

"Tomorrow night then," the woman said. "Midnight at the stables."

A secret midnight meeting! Thrills upon thrills!

"If you're sure it will be safe," the woman continued.

"Nobody goes near the stables at night," said Lord Evesham. "The only risk is transporting it. Are you sure the van's roadworthy? We can't risk it breaking down and some nosy policeman looking in the back. It's the key to the success of the whole operation."

Operation? Policeman? This wasn't sounding so much like a romance any more.

"The van's very reliable," said the woman, "and even if it did break down – which it won't – I'm perfectly capable of mending it myself, as you know full well. I'll see you tomorrow at midnight."

She turned towards the front of the house, and Lord Evesham walked off in the opposite direction.

Sidney walked back across the rose garden, her heart beating fast. So this woman was bringing something to the stables tomorrow at midnight. Something that Lord Evesham was very anxious to keep secret.

What could it be, and what was the operation to which it was the key? Was it connected with the war? Or were they smuggling something illegal? Sidney had no idea, but she knew one thing for certain. At midnight tomorrow she would be keeping watch over the stable block from her bedroom window.

# CHAPTER NINE

# What If?

Nancy scooped up a heap of muddy riding clothes from Lord Evesham's dressing-room floor and stuffed them into a laundry bag.

*Filthy slob*, she thought. She'd have been walloped if she'd left her room in that state. One law for the rich and one for the poor, as Florence would say.

She hadn't seen Lord Evesham since the day she'd arrived. The housemaids' schedule was designed so they'd be invisible to the family, just as Florence had said. But she now knew that he worked for the Air Ministry, and that had eased her mind about the conversation she'd overheard between him and Dorothy Taylor. They must be doing some kind of undercover work for the Secret Service, defeating Nazi spies or something like that. He was clearly trying to protect Dorothy Taylor from taking risks, but it was typical of her bravery to laugh in the face of danger. Nancy felt a bit guilty about eavesdropping on their conversation, but it was very exciting to know something nobody else did. And it was a wonderful feeling that she was keeping Dorothy

Taylor's secrets.

She slung the laundry bag over her shoulder and took her cleaning box to the first-floor housemaids' closet. It was hard to keep her mind on work today. She kept thinking about the letter she'd received from her mother that morning.

"We've had no news of Jack yet," Mother had written. "Everyone in the village is in a terrible state of nerves, asking each other if their husbands or sons are back in England. Dad has joined the Local Defence Volunteers. I don't know how much use he'll be, with his lungs, but he feels better knowing he's doing his bit to protect us all if the Germans invade. They're to be issued with tin helmets and LDV armbands, and in due course they'll have weapons and uniforms. They'll have training every week and their job will be to hold back invading troops until the regular army gets there."

This made Nancy feel even worse. Now her dad *and* her brother would be fighting the Germans.

As she opened the door of the housemaids' closet, she saw Rosa curled up on the floor, crying. A letter lay beside her.

Nancy dropped the box and the laundry bag, a cold feeling in the pit of her stomach. Rosa was constantly worried about her aunts and cousins back in Austria.

"Rosa, what's wrong?"

Rosa carried on crying. Nancy's legs felt weak with dread. She sat down beside her and touched her arm.

"What's wrong?" she asked again.

She waited until Rosa's sobs had calmed.

"It's my brother," she said, wiping her eyes.

Nancy's heart beat very fast. "What's happened?"

"He's been interned," said Rosa. "Arrested by two policemen and taken away. Poor Walter, who's never done anything wrong, arrested!"

"But why?" asked Nancy, relieved that at least he was alive. Walter had been at university in Vienna, but now he was working in a tailoring factory in the East End of London.

"Because he's an enemy alien. Just because we're Austrian. We were classified as friendly enemy aliens because we're refugees from Nazi persecution, but now they're arresting us too. His friends at the factory told the police they'd made a mistake, but they said they had to follow orders. The government is so frightened of spies that they are locking up all Germans and Austrians. Maybe they will come for my poor parents next!"

In Vienna, Rosa's father had been a successful accountant, but now her parents were working as servants in London, living in their employer's attic.

"Do you know where they've taken Walter?" Nancy asked.

"No, they wouldn't say. My mother rang the police, but they said he's no longer in their charge and they weren't allowed to tell her where he was. He's not even allowed to receive or send messages." She put her head in her hands and sobbed.

"I'm so sorry," Nancy said, feeling how pathetically inadequate her words were. "I'm sure they'll let him out soon, once they realise they've made a mistake."

"They won't let him out," sobbed Rosa. "Some people were interned for the whole of the last war. He might be locked up for years. And when I'm sixteen they'll lock me up too."

"Why don't you go back to bed?" Nancy said. "You're not fit to work today. I'll do the dowager's rooms once I've finished his lordship's."

Rosa shook her head and wiped her eyes with her sleeve. "No, I need to work. If I go to bed I will only cry, and what help will that be?"

"Well, if you're sure. But if you do want to go back to bed, let me know."

She squeezed Rosa's arm and stood up, filled with anger and a horrible feeling of powerlessness. Millions of people's lives were being ruined by this awful war, all because of one man's crazed desire for power.

She lugged the dirty washing down the servants' stairs and over to the laundry rooms behind the stable yard. Before the war there had been full-time laundry maids at Stanbrook, Florence had told her, but they had left and, as with all the other staff, they hadn't been replaced. So now the housemaids left the dirty linen in the laundry room and Mr Burford took it to the village laundry in the pony and trap.

As Nancy crossed the stable yard, she caught a whiff of a familiar smell. It was the same smell that clung to the laundry she was carrying. Lord Evesham's cigarette smoke. But she couldn't see his lordship.

She walked through the narrow passage on the corner, between the stable block where the horses were housed and the disused, padlocked stables in the other block. At the back of the stables, a big ginger tom cat basked in the sun. Nancy had made friends with him a couple of days ago, and he loved having his tummy tickled. She crouched down by the warm brick wall to stroke him. He rolled on to his side, and she was about to say "Good boy" when she heard a voice.

The small grimy window high up in the stable wall was slightly ajar. Nancy made out the low murmur of men's voices. One was his lordship's. She didn't recognise the other.

"Are you sure we won't be overheard?" asked the unknown voice.

"Stop fussing, Lonsdale," said his lordship. "Albert's working in the gardens and Burford's taken my mother out. The place is deserted."

"It sounds as though her mission was entirely successful," murmured the man called Lonsdale.

"Yes, it all worked perfectly."

"And your trip to Ireland? Is that going ahead?"

"All arranged for the twenty-first," said Lord Evesham. He dropped his voice further, so that Nancy had to strain to hear it. "I've gathered almost all the information I need, so I can personally hand everything over to the German delegation."

Nancy frowned. Handing information to the Germans?

"Dorothy did well," Lord Evesham was saying,

"but it's far too risky to attempt anything like that on a large scale. Much more efficient to attack from the air."

Dorothy? Were they talking about Dorothy Taylor?

"They'll strike soon, I imagine," said Lonsdale.

"No doubt about it," said Lord Evesham. "France will surrender any day now, and then Hitler will turn his attention here. Once he's destroyed our air defences, it will all be over very quickly."

Nancy had heard other people express this opinion, and they always sounded deeply gloomy at the prospect. But Lord Evesham sounded oddly cheerful.

"Well, it's about time the country was run by the aristocracy again and we got rid of this failed attempt at democracy," said Lonsdale.

"Democracy!" scoffed Lord Evesham. "What a disaster that's been. Giving the vote to servants and farmhands, as though they're capable of forming an opinion on how the country's run. Never heard such nonsense."

A horse snorted loudly from a nearby stable.

"Fancy taking the hunters out for a spot of exercise?" said Lord Evesham.

"Absolutely."

A door scraped open. Nancy grabbed the bag and ran on tiptoe to the laundry room. She sank down on the tiled floor, her back to the wall, heart thumping.

Lord Evesham was going to Ireland to hand over information to the Germans. But wasn't it illegal to communicate with the enemy? Was that why they were muttering so furtively?

No, Lord Evesham couldn't possibly be a traitor. He worked at the very top of the Air Ministry. Perhaps men at that level had to communicate with the Germans. Or perhaps he was working with Germans who were trying to bring down Hitler. She knew there were people in Germany who hated what Hitler was doing. Some of them had even tried to kill him.

Or perhaps Lord Evesham was feeding *false* information to the Germans. The Secret Service was bound to be trying to mislead Hitler about Britain's war plans.

Yes, that made a lot of sense, now she thought about it.

She wondered what the men were talking about when they mentioned Dorothy. Of course, they might have been talking about a different Dorothy. It was a common enough name.

It was strange, Nancy thought, what they had said about getting rid of democracy. That was what the fascists wanted too.

But then, a lot of aristocrats probably thought like that. They were bound to think the country would be a better place if they ran it.

She felt slightly uneasy as she remembered the constant reminders on the wireless and in the newspapers to report anything suspicious. Was this suspicious? Should she report it?

But Lord Evesham was a war hero. He wouldn't

do anything treacherous.

*No, Nancy,* she told herself. *They were obviously discussing something you don't understand. Just keep your mouth shut and stay well away from things that don't concern you.*

# CHAPTER TEN

## Midnight at
## the Stables

Sidney's main concern was the life of her torch battery. She was perfectly happy to stay awake until midnight reading *The Murder of Roger Ackroyd* under the bedclothes, but she didn't know what she would do if the battery ran out.

By half past eleven it was getting quite feeble, so she decided to switch it off and start watching the stable block. Very slowly, in case the bedsprings creaked, she inched her way out of bed and kneeled at the open window, her elbows propped on the sill. She glanced back at the others, but they hadn't stirred. Ginny was snoring gently.

Once her eyes grew used to the shadowy moonlight, Sidney could make out the outlines of the stable block well enough to see any movement. Apart from the occasional hooting of a tawny owl, Stanbrook was silent. She watched and waited. A bat flew past, and then another. The clock on the roof of the stable block chimed once. Quarter to twelve.

Through the trees that lined the drive, Sidney noticed a dim light moving slowly towards the house.

Her heartbeat sped up as the light drew closer, and she heard the low sound of an engine. It was really happening!

As the vehicle approached the front of the house, Sidney saw it was a large van. It trundled at a snail's pace across the gravel and through the archway into the stable yard. The driver turned the van round so its back doors faced a stable door on the far side of the yard.

The lights and engine turned off. Sidney waited for the driver to get out, but the doors stayed shut. The silence was overwhelming.

She suddenly felt very uncomfortable. What was going on at Stanbrook? What was in that van?

A figure appeared through the trees behind the stable yard. Goosebumps prickled on Sidney's arms. The silhouette looked like a man; it must be Lord Evesham.

The man walked over to the van and stopped at the driver's door. It opened and somebody got out. They were about the same height as Lord Evesham, and wearing trousers. Sidney couldn't be sure it was the woman she had seen yesterday, but who else would it be?

Bedsprings creaked behind her. She whipped her head round, her heart thumping.

It was only Phyllis turning in her sleep. Anyway, even if one of the others did wake and see her looking out of the window, she could just say she'd woken up and needed some fresh air.

When she turned back, the back doors of the van

were open. Lord Evesham opened the stable door and both people climbed into the back of the van. They carried something out and laid it on the ground, then disappeared into the van again.

There was a slight rumbling and squeaking, and then they reappeared, either side of a large bulky object that looked as though it was draped in a cloth. They manoeuvred the object slowly down some sort of ramp. Presumably the ramp had been what they had placed on the ground earlier.

Whatever they were moving must be on wheels, because they trundled it into the stable without lifting it. Or perhaps they had put it on a trolley with castors to move it more easily. That was how the new piano at home had been brought into the house.

If it was on a trolley, that meant it was something heavy, or delicate, or both.

What could it be?

The two figures emerged from the stable. The woman closed the van's back doors and opened the driver's door.

Lord Evesham spent quite a long time closing the stable door. He must be locking it, Sidney thought. Well, of course he was. He was hardly likely to leave it unlocked when he was hiding something so secret and crucial.

The van's engine rumbled into life and the dimmed lights came on. The van trundled very slowly out of the stable yard, and Lord Evesham disappeared through the trees. Stanbrook settled back into shadows and silence.

Sidney sat cross-legged on her bed, her heart beating very fast. How utterly thrilling this was. But also how baffling. She was no closer to understanding what was going on than she had been before.

Were they smuggling goods of some sort? But Lord Evesham was hugely rich. Why would he need to make money by smuggling?

No, it must be something to do with the war effort. After all, he was very high up in the Air Ministry. He was probably involved in some sort of secret operation to defeat the Germans. Perhaps they had been bringing in code-breaking equipment. It seemed a bit odd that he would keep it in a stable at Stanbrook, but there were probably all sorts of things going on behind the scenes that ordinary people knew nothing about.

If she were a character in one of her detective stories, Sidney thought, she would find a way to get into that stable and see for herself what was there. But that was all very well in fiction. In real life it would be far too risky.

Still, she thought, with a tingle of excitement, wouldn't it be the most enormous fun to try?

# CHAPTER ELEVEN

## An Overactive Imagination

In the library, Nancy furiously rubbed beeswax into the earl's dining table. She had put far too much polish on the cloth and now the wood was covered in waxy smears. It would take forever to get rid of them.

"Are you all right?" asked Rosa, who was dusting the bookshelves. "You look as though you're fighting the table, not polishing it."

"I'm fine," said Nancy.

If only she *could* fight somebody. She needed some way of relieving the tension. It was over twenty-four hours since she had heard that disturbing conversation between Lord Evesham and the unknown Mr Lonsdale, and she still couldn't decide what to do about it.

Of course Lord Evesham almost certainly had a top-secret job that she knew nothing about. There was probably nothing suspicious at all in what he'd said.

Deep down, though, she knew that the real reason she wasn't reporting it was cowardice. At best, she would be laughed out of the police station. At worst, what if the police told Lord Evesham what she'd said, and she was sacked?

But her brother and countless other men were risking their lives every day fighting the Nazis. Surely the least she could do was report what she had heard. Just in case there was anything in it.

The image came back into her head of her brother huddled on a Dunkirk beach with thousands of other soldiers, waiting to be rescued while the Germans bombed them from the air. There had been nothing in the post again this morning. The longer the silence, the worse his chances must be.

*Stop it, Nancy*, she told herself. *Think about someone else's problems for a change.*

"Have you heard any more about your brother?" she asked Rosa.

Rosa's face tensed with emotion. "Nothing. It's so stupid! Why can't they see that? Walter wants to fight Hitler, not help him! What was the point of coming to England to be locked up in camps? That's what we thought we were escaping from. If all the Jews are thrown into camps here, and then the Germans come, it will be as bad as if we had stayed in Vienna."

Nancy turned cold as she remembered Lord Evesham's words. *France will surrender any day now, and then Hitler will turn his attention here.*

Suddenly she remembered something Mr Armitage had said at breakfast the other day. "If you see or hear anything suspicious," he had told the servants, "report it to me, and I will take the appropriate action."

Her stomach churned at the thought of telling him what she had heard. He wouldn't hear a word against Lord Evesham. How on earth would he react?

But at least it wouldn't be her responsibility any longer. She could pass the burden to the butler, and he could decide what to do about it.

She wouldn't mention Dorothy Taylor, though. Nancy couldn't bear the thought of her name being connected with anything suspicious. Even if, as was almost certainly the case, there was nothing in it at all.

Lunch was delicious, as always, but Nancy found it hard to eat. She needed to tell Mr Armitage as soon as the meal was over. If she waited any longer, her courage might drain away.

She was so agitated that she knocked over her water glass, and then knocked over Rosa's as she was mopping up the mess.

"What on earth is the matter with you, Nancy?" snapped Mrs Dawes, the cook.

"Sorry," said Nancy. "I'm really sorry."

At the end of the meal Mr Armitage cleared his throat, which always meant he was about to make an announcement.

"His lordship has informed me," he said, "that he will be hosting an important dinner on the Thursday after next."

"How many guests?" asked Mrs Dawes.

"Fourteen."

"Fourteen!"

"It is a centuries-old tradition that, when a new Earl of Stanbrook inherits the earldom, he hosts a dinner for the most prominent figures in the county. The lord-lieutenant of Oxfordshire and a number of landowners and dignitaries will be attending: Members of Parliament, the high sheriff, the chief constable and so on."

"And how am I expected to cater for this dinner with things the way they are at the moment?"

"I am sure you will find a way to work miracles, as you always do, Mrs Dawes."

After lunch, Nancy lingered, her stomach churning, until only Mr Armitage was left in the servants' hall.

"Excuse me," she said. "Could I speak to you for a moment, please?"

"What is it, Nancy?"

"There's something I need to report. I was taking some clothes to the laundry and I accidentally overheard a conversation his lordship was having in the stables with a man called Lonsdale."

The butler drew his brows together. His eyes seemed to have darkened.

"I wasn't meaning to listen," Nancy said, not entirely truthfully, "but I couldn't help hearing. His lordship said he'd been gathering information and is going to Ireland on the twenty-first to personally hand over information to the Germans. I didn't know exactly what he meant, but you said we should report anything suspicious, sir."

Mr Armitage made a startled sound. Nancy hurried on before he could interrupt.

"He said France will soon surrender and Hitler will turn his attention to Britain. Then he said Germany will destroy our air defences and the war will be over very quickly."

To her astonishment, a little smile was playing at the corners of the butler's mouth.

"Oh, Nancy," he said with an amused shake of his head, "you clearly have an overactive imagination. I know you mean well, but I'm afraid you've put two and two together and made five."

His patronising tone made Nancy itch with frustration. "But it's what I heard! I didn't make it up."

"I don't doubt that you overheard a conversation, Nancy, and that in itself is a very grave matter. I had assumed you were well brought up, but it appears I was wrong."

Nancy opened her mouth to protest, but he held up his hand for silence.

"And, quite apart from the moral aspect," he continued, "the danger of eavesdropping is that you are almost certain to misinterpret what you hear. His lordship deals with very important matters of government that you couldn't possibly understand."

"But I know it's illegal to communicate with the enemy."

Mr Armitage nodded solemnly. "It is indeed illegal for us ordinary people, but those in positions of great power and responsibility have to carry out all sorts of highly sensitive work that we are not even aware of. You know, I am sure, about his lordship's distinguished record in the last war, and his extraordinary flying achievements. He is now using his expertise to carry out vital service in the Air Ministry. We should all be extremely proud to serve such a man."

Nancy nodded. She felt as though a weight had been lifted from her chest. Of course ordinary people like her wouldn't know how the war was being conducted behind the scenes. There must be so much that was top secret, as she had suspected. She was glad she'd mentioned it, though. This had gone much better than she'd expected. Mr Armitage wasn't even angry.

"I fear, Nancy," the butler continued, "that you have been reading too much fiction. There is a great danger of overstimulation in a mind such as yours."

Nancy stared at him. A mind such as hers? What was he saying?

"An overactive imagination is sadly a common fault in young girls. If it were not for the fact that you are a very good worker, I would seriously consider dismissing you. As it is, you may have one more chance, on the condition that there is to be no more reading of novels. They are damaging your brain and making you hysterical. Is that understood?"

"Yes, sir," she said, with no intention of obeying him. How would he even know if she was reading a novel? It wasn't as though she did it in working hours.

"Go and fetch the book you brought with you," he said.

Nancy stared at him in horror. "Oh, please don't take my book, sir."

"I will not repeat my request," he said.

Without another word, Nancy walked out of the kitchen and stomped up the back stairs. How could he take away her most prized possession?

*Jane Eyre* had been her school leaving prize. Inside the front cover the headmaster had written: *Awarded to Nancy Robson, for Reading, Writing and Recitation*. Nancy loved reading, but all her other books came from the library. *Jane Eyre* was the only book she'd ever owned, and Mr Armitage was taking it from her before she'd even had the chance to finish it.

Feet came clattering down the stairs above her.

"Have you learned the spellings yet, Lucinda?"

"No, when's the test?"

"Next lesson. They're awfully tricky and Miss Verney said she'll give detentions to anybody who gets less than sixteen out of twenty."

"I'll copy your answers," said Lucinda. "I haven't had time to learn them."

"They're all double-letter ones," said another voice, "and I can never get those right. Does 'accommodation' have two cs or two ms? And what about 'committee'?"

"Two ms, I think," said the first girl. "It's the ones with silent letters and heaps of consonants all jumbled together that I'm hopeless at. How is anybody supposed to spell 'psychology'?"

They rounded the bend, taking up the whole width of the staircase. Nancy flattened herself against the wall, but a girl barged right into her. Nancy grabbed her arm to stop herself tumbling down the stairs.

"Get your hands off me, you filthy creature!" said the girl. Nancy could tell from her voice that it was the one called Lucinda.

"You almost pushed me down the stairs!" Nancy said. "I could have broken my neck."

"Then you'd have deserved it. How dare you stand in my way? If you were working in my father's house, you'd be dismissed for that."

With a final look of contempt, she continued down the stairs, followed by her friends.

"By the way," Nancy called after them, "'accommodation' has two cs and two ms. 'Committee' has two ms and two ts. And 'psychology' is spelled 'p-s-y-c-h-o-l-o-g-y'."

They turned and stared.

"Ignore her," said Lucinda, as she rounded the next bend. "She's making it up. Nasty common thing."

# CHAPTER TWELVE

# Snooping Around

"Copy down this title, girls," said Miss Verney, writing on the blackboard in her spiky script. "You have twenty minutes to compose your answer."

The Upper Fourth's form room was a pretty drawing room on the ground floor. The crystal chandelier still hung from the ceiling, but the furniture had been replaced with school desks and chairs. Blackout blinds were fixed to the elegant windows, and a blackboard on an easel stood in front of the marble fireplace.

Sidney looked at the essay title. *Explain, as carefully as you can, how you would lay the table for luncheon at home.*

How did Miss Verney manage to think up such utterly boring subjects? It must have taken her hours to come up with something that tedious.

"What an idiotic title," murmured Lucinda, who sat with Ginny at the desk behind Sidney's. "Why would I ever need to lay my own table?"

Then she leaned forward and murmured, "I expect you'll find it useful, though, won't you, new girl?

I imagine you'll always have to lay your own table."

Sidney pretended she hadn't heard. It would be nice, she thought, to invite Lucinda for luncheon at home. She would serve a delicious soup containing a generous helping of an undetectable poison, one that would guarantee a slow, agonising death. As Lucinda thrashed about in paroxysms of agony, stretching out her hands in a desperate plea for help, Sidney would calmly butter her bread and observe Lucinda's death throes with a sympathetic smile.

Miss Verney was handing back last week's essays. They had been given the title "A Walk in the Woods".

The teacher dropped Phyllis's essay on her desk.

"Not quite as weak as your previous effort, Phyllis. Although it might have achieved a higher mark had you spent more time describing the landscape and less time describing the horse."

Sidney stored up this remark to tell George in her next letter. She gazed out of the window, thinking about what she had seen last night. Could she tell George about that?

"Sidney Dashworth, you haven't written a word."

Miss Verney was standing beside her desk, holding the marked essays. Sidney recognised hers on the top of the pile. She had written a murder mystery story inspired by the detective novels she'd read from her father's collection. She strongly suspected that it would not be to Miss Verney's taste, but she had enjoyed writing it too much to care.

"Sorry, madam," she said. "I was thinking."

"Given the quality of your work," said Miss

Verney, "I find that very hard to believe."

Lucinda tittered and Miss Verney gave her a warm smile. She picked up Sidney's murder story between her thumb and forefinger as though it was a particularly unpleasant piece of litter.

"It appears, Miss Dashworth, that any thinking you manage to do is of a most regrettable variety. I gave you the title 'A Walk in the Woods'. It was an invitation to meditate upon the beauty of nature, not to describe a gruesome death. It would seem that you have been granted access to the most unsuitable reading material at home."

She dropped the paper on Sidney's desk. The entire story had been crossed out in red ink.

"Which book did you bring to school this term?" she asked.

"*The Murder of Roger Ackroyd*, madam."

Miss Verney looked as disgusted as if Sidney had murdered Roger Ackroyd herself.

"I see. Filling your mind with vulgar trash, instead of taking this precious opportunity to acquaint yourself with the treasures of English literature. Well, the *book* –" she said the word as though it had invisible quotation marks around it – "shall, of course, be confiscated, and you will no longer be permitted to read fiction. It is clearly having a detrimental effect on your mind. From now on, I shall select suitable reading material for you myself."

Sidney stared at her in horror. Lucinda sniggered as the teacher walked away. Sidney turned round to face her. It would be good to give Lucinda something to think about.

"Do you know how Lord Evesham's first wife died?" Sidney whispered.

Lucinda looked startled.

"Was it perhaps a sudden, unexplained death?" Sidney asked. "Because I happen to know there's more to Lord Evesham than meets the eye."

Ginny looked at her curiously, but Lucinda curled her upper lip in a sneer. "You're such a freak," she hissed. "Even Miss Verney's noticed it."

Sidney gave her what she hoped was a knowing look. "I'd be *extremely* careful if I were you. I happen to know that Lord Evesham is hiding some pretty big secrets."

It was prep time before Sidney had the chance to slip away unnoticed. As luck would have it, the prefect supervising their form that evening was famously dreamy and unobservant, so it was easy for Sidney to wait until Joan was deep in study, and then mutter to Phyllis that she needed the lavatory. She left the room and walked out on to the terrace. She had to duck below the windowsills to avoid being seen as she passed the Lower Fifth's form room. As soon as she reached the corner of the house, she hurried across to the stable block.

The stables were quiet and there was nobody in sight. The stable where Lord Evesham and the woman had put the mysterious object last night was padlocked. The lock looked new.

Sidney's heartbeat quickened. She glanced around

again, then pulled a grip from her hair. People in detective novels were always picking locks with hairgrips.

She pulled the two sides of the grip apart until they were at a ninety-degree angle, and then tried to push it into the lock. Blast. The little rubber piece on the end was too big to fit in. She would have to pull it off.

"Can I help you?" asked a soft voice behind her.

Sidney jumped as though she'd had an electric shock. She turned to see Lord Evesham facing her from a few yards away. He wore riding clothes and held a whip.

"Oh, g-good afternoon, Your Highness, I mean, your lordship," she stammered, clutching the bent pin so tightly that it dug into her hand. Was she supposed to curtsy?

"Can I be of assistance?" he asked gently, looking intently at her. "Are you lost? The stable block is out of bounds to schoolgirls. Did your headmistress fail to inform you of that fact?"

His eyes were locked on her. Sidney's insides felt like they'd turned to water. She could claim she'd wanted to look at the horses, but he wouldn't believe that for a second. He must have seen exactly what she was doing.

"Er, I ... I... That is, my friends and I... We were looking for a place to have a secret club, and we thought this would be an awfully jolly place to have it, your lordship, sir."

Awfully jolly? Why was she speaking like a

character in a story?

Lord Evesham said nothing. With his eyes fixed on her, he held the whip in his right hand, tapping it softly into the palm of his left hand.

Sidney crumbled. "I'm so sorry, sir," she said. "I don't know what came over me. It was a terrible thing to do. I should never have come here. I'm so sorry."

"What is your name?" he asked quietly.

"I... My..." It flashed across her mind to say "Lucinda Gore-Withers", but while that would be immensely satisfying in the short term, it would inevitably end up getting her into more trouble than she would be already.

"Sidney Dashworth," she muttered.

He took a step towards her. Every muscle in her body clenched. What was he going to do?

"Sidney Dashworth," he murmured. "Well, if I were you, Sidney Dashworth, I would keep to the limits of the school in future. It's really not the done thing to trespass on private property. And I'm afraid we shouldn't be able to guarantee your safety if you were to be caught snooping around the outbuildings again."

He paused. Then he said, "Have I made myself quite clear?"

"Yes, sir," murmured Sidney, her teeth chattering. "Quite clear."

She heard footsteps and whistling, and a boy appeared from the path between the stable blocks, swinging a bucket. It was the boy who'd told her about the secret passage. She had never been so pleased to see anyone in her life.

"A pleasure to meet you, Sidney Dashworth," said Lord Evesham in a friendly, relaxed tone. "I shan't forget our little encounter. Now, you had probably better run along to your lessons, don't you think?"

"Yes, sir," muttered Sidney, and she stumbled back across the cobbles, her legs cold and shaking.

One thing was obvious. Lord Evesham was hiding something very important in that stable. Something he really didn't want to be discovered.

# CHAPTER THIRTEEN

# What If He Was Wrong?

The following morning, another letter from Nancy's mother was sitting on the breakfast table. Nancy opened it quickly, before she could be overcome by hope or fear.

"Still no news of Jack," her mother wrote. "Your dad's going half mad with worry."

Nancy was gripped by a cold dread that seeped through her whole body. But no news was good news, she told herself.

"Most people have heard by now that their boys are back," her mother continued. "Mrs Wilson heard that Tony's safe, and the Youngs found out Roy's in a hospital down south. Jean's going to see him today. I'll write and tell you as soon as we hear. I hope you're keeping well and cheerful."

Agnes, the scullery maid, looked up from her newspaper. "Look at this. Three hundred Nazi warplanes dropped a thousand bombs on Paris yesterday. They even bombed schools, the evil swine. Ten children killed, poor little mites."

"It's disgusting," said Florence. "Poor France,

how much longer can they hold out with the Nazis bombing them like that?"

"Thank goodness we've got the Channel keeping Hitler at bay," said Agnes. "Else he'd be sending his tanks into England any minute now."

"That's why they'll invade by air instead," said Florence. "And they'll try to destroy our Air Force first. Those poor brave boys in the RAF."

"Have you seen they've put obstacles on the village green to stop enemy planes from landing?" said Agnes.

"What sort of obstacles?" asked Nancy.

"Like wigwams, made from long poles. The farmers are all putting obstacles in their fields too – rusty old ploughs, stuff like that."

"Shouldn't we have them here too then?" asked Florence. "In the park? There's plenty of space here for enemy planes to land."

"Mrs Simms at the Post Office said Fred what works on the estate said the Warden asked his lordship and his lordship said it would spoil the look of the park."

There was an awkward silence round the table. Butterflies fluttered in Nancy's stomach. Had Lord Evesham refused to put obstacles to enemy planes on his land because they would spoil the look of the park? Or was it for a more sinister reason?

The conversation she'd overheard played in her head again.

*France will surrender any day now, and then Hitler will turn his attention here. Once he's destroyed our air defences, it will all be over very quickly.*

*It's about time the country was run by the aristocracy again and we got rid of this failed attempt at democracy.*

Naturally Mr Armitage couldn't imagine the possibility of his employer betraying his country. But what if he was wrong? Should she report what she had heard to a higher authority?

She couldn't keep her worries to herself any longer. She would telephone the police today, before she could change her mind again. Then they could decide what to do about it, and she would have done her duty.

Of course Mrs Dawes chose that afternoon to find a pile of fiddly mending for her. Because they were so short-staffed, Mrs Dawes was housekeeper as well as cook, and she considered it part of her job to keep the female staff busy with sewing when things were quiet in the house.

"Can I do it tomorrow, please?" Nancy asked. "I've got some errands to run in the village."

"Well, stop complaining, and you'll get it finished quicker."

Nancy was finished by three, and she bolted across the courtyard at the same time as the schoolgirls were filing out on to the West Lawn for one of their ridiculous drilling classes. They must have so many clothes, she thought. They seemed to wear a different outfit for every activity.

She found herself stuck behind that awful Lucinda

and her hangers-on, walking four abreast and blocking her way.

"I wish we didn't have drill," Lucinda was saying. "I need to practise that ghastly Shakespeare speech."

"Oh yes, it's your turn to recite today, isn't it?" said one of the others. "Have you learned it?"

"I tried, but it's so dull, it doesn't sink in."

She began to recite.

"'The quality of mercy is not strained;
It falleth as the gentle rain from heaven'."

"Droppeth," corrected Nancy.

They turned round. When they saw the housemaid, they looked dumbfounded. Lucinda tossed her head and quickened her pace as she began the speech again.

"'The quality of mercy is not strained;
It falleth as the gentle rain from heaven
On the … upon the…'"

She flung up her arms dramatically. "You see. It doesn't sink in. If he'd written anything that made sense—"

"'Upon the place beneath'," said Nancy.

The schoolgirls turned again and stared at her.

"Will you be quiet?" snapped Lucinda.

"Just trying to help," said Nancy. "'It droppeth as the gentle rain from heaven upon the place beneath.' That's the next line of Portia's speech."

They gaped. Lucinda opened her mouth, and shut it again. She turned and sped up. Nancy followed them, reciting the rest of the speech as she walked.

Lucinda hurried through the garden gate, followed

by the others. Nancy raised her eyebrows and turned to walk down the drive, feeling ten feet tall. What a piece of luck that her school play last year had been *The Merchant of Venice*!

As she approached the bend, she heard an engine. She stepped on to the verge just in time to avoid a motorcycle speeding up the drive in a cloud of dust. The motorcyclist wore a leather jacket, goggles, boots and breeches, and she had shingled blonde hair and bright red lipstick.

Dorothy Taylor! She must be coming to visit Lord Evesham.

Nancy's stomach squirmed as she remembered that strange conversation. It was all so confusing. It would be a relief to report it to the police. Perhaps they would be able to make sense of it.

# CHAPTER FOURTEEN

# News

The signpost at the crossroads had been taken down by order of the government, so that invading Germans wouldn't be able to find their way around. As she came in sight of the village green, Nancy saw the wigwam-like structures that Agnes had been talking about. Well, if enemy planes couldn't land here, then presumably they would land in the vast open acres of Stanbrook Park. She shivered at the thought of Nazi warplanes on the lawns, unloading swastika-wearing soldiers with machine guns.

A line of exhausted-looking children with gas masks slung over their shoulders followed a woman across the green towards the village hall. The children carried cases and had labels round their necks. Poor little things. Thousands of children were being sent out of London every day now that invasion was expected at any minute.

The public telephone box was on the corner of the village green. Nancy had rarely used the telephone, so she concentrated hard on remembering what to do. She could have just walked into the police station, of course, but if they saw how young she was, they would be even less likely to take her seriously.

She put her two pennies in the box, listened for the dialling tone and pressed the button when she heard the operator's voice.

Her stomach churned as she waited to be connected. There was a click, and then a voice said, "Stanbrook Police Station, Sergeant Bell speaking."

Nancy felt sick with nerves. "Oh, erm, hello. Erm, I need to report something suspicious."

"Go on."

"Er, I work at Stanbrook House, and I overheard a conversation between Lord Evesham and another man, and Lord Evesham said he was gathering information and going to Ireland on the twenty-first of June to hand it over to the Germans."

She paused, waiting for a reaction. The sergeant was silent, and Nancy wondered whether she had been cut off.

"Hello?" she said. "Did you hear me?"

"Now look here, young lady," said the sergeant. "I've just about had enough of your sort making prank calls. Should be ashamed of yourselves, you should. I had two kids send me on a wild goose chase yesterday, searching for a parachutist that didn't exist. Your mates, were they? All part of the same gang?"

"No!" said Nancy. "This isn't a prank call, I promise. I can tell you more details."

"Oh yes, I bet you've got plenty of details. So did those kids yesterday. Dressed as a nun, he was, they said, but carrying a haversack with a swastika embroidered on it. Sound familiar?"

"Sir, I promise this isn't a joke. Lord Evesham said he doesn't believe in democracy. I think you might need to investigate him, sir."

There was a pause. Then, in a different tone, the sergeant said, "You work at Stanbrook House, you say? What was your name again?"

Nancy turned cold. She slammed the phone on its receiver and raced back up the lane, occasionally glancing behind her, fully expecting to see a police officer in hot pursuit. She only slowed down when she was halfway up the drive.

Why, oh why, had she said she worked at Stanbrook House? How could she have been so stupid? What if the police telephoned Mr Armitage to report the call? He would know immediately it was her, and she would lose her job.

The trouble was, she had no evidence to back up her concerns. It was probably nothing, but surely somebody should at least investigate?

She stopped and drew in her breath. Of course! She could investigate herself! She cleaned Lord Evesham's rooms. If he was hiding secret information, then she was in the perfect position to find it. She would start looking straight away.

As she walked past the entrance to the stable yard, she saw that horrible Lucinda again, standing outside the stable of Lord Evesham's enormous hunter. The horse was looking out of the upper half of the stable door. Lucinda held out her hand, offering him an apple core. He stretched his neck towards it and she gave a little yelp, leaped backwards and dropped the apple. Nancy shook her head in contempt and glanced at the stable clock. Good, she wasn't due back at work for another half an hour. She couldn't bear to go into the house yet. She needed to walk and think.

She made her way to the South Lawn in front of the Long Gallery, with its statues shrouded in dust sheets. Albert knelt on the other side of the lawn, weeding the rose beds.

"Nancy!" came a shout.

Nancy turned to see Rosa running towards her, waving a letter. She froze in dread.

"I've been looking everywhere for you," Rosa said. "This came in the afternoon post."

Nancy stared at her mother's handwriting, her heart thumping in terror. Then she ripped open the envelope and unfolded the letter. Rosa stood in silence.

"Oh!" Nancy gasped. "He's back!"

"Oh, Nancy, that's wonderful!" cried Rosa.

"He's back!" repeated Nancy, tears filling her eyes. "He's safe! Oh, thank goodness, thank goodness."

She started laughing from sheer joy. Jack was safe! He was safe and on his way home.

"That's so wonderful," said Rosa again.

"I can't believe it!" said Nancy, flooded with such lightness that she felt she could float away like a balloon on a breeze. "Oh, I'm so happy!" She gave

Rosa a huge hug.

Rosa hugged her back, laughing. "I'm so glad for you."

They turned at the sound of a squeak. The orchard gate opened and Lord Evesham appeared with Dorothy Taylor.

"Look," whispered Rosa. "Your heroine."

"Yes," said Nancy, wishing she could feel as joyful at the sight of Dorothy Taylor as she had on her first day.

Miss Taylor seemed struck by the sight of Albert weeding the roses. She frowned as she watched him. Then she glanced across at the maids and gave Rosa a strangely piercing look.

What did it mean?

Like so much else at Stanbrook, Nancy could make no sense of it at all.

# CHAPTER FIFTEEN

# A Gallery
of Ghosts

Dear Dordy

I wonder if you know you have a sister still living in England? Rumour has it she's mouldering away in an ancient haunted house in the depths of Oxfordshire, knitting sadly misshapen socks, desperate for a kind word from her cruelly neglectful brother.

"Have you still not heard from your brother, Sidney?" Ginny asked when they were stripping their beds the following Tuesday.

Sidney shook her head. "No, but he's terrible at writing, and I expect he's terrifically busy shooting down German planes and things."

Lucinda pulled a concerned face. "Oh dear, I'm terribly sorry."

Sidney gave her pillow a violent shake. "Sorry about what?"

"Well, if you haven't heard anything yet, I imagine it's bad news. All the relatives of the men who've come back have heard by now."

Sidney's insides felt hollow. *Stop it*, she told herself.

*She's trying to poison your mind. Don't let her.*

"Shut up, Lucinda!" said Ginny. "That's an awful thing to say."

"Don't speak to me like that," snapped Lucinda. "Just because you're in love with her precious brother."

"I'm not in love with him!" protested Ginny, her face scarlet.

"Yes, you are. Just from seeing a photograph, for heaven's sake. You really are pathetic."

"Oh, stop being vile, Lucinda," said Sidney.

Lucinda swung round, her eyes dark with anger. "Don't you tell me what I can and can't say, new girl. Nobody even likes you."

Sidney raised her eyebrows. "And you think they like *you*?"

Lucinda's face went rigid. She picked up the glass of water by her bed. "Excuse me, this is stale. I'm going to tip it out of the window."

She walked towards Sidney's bed. As she reached her chair, she flicked her wrist and tipped the water over the photograph of George. Ginny and Phyllis gasped in horror.

"Stop it!" shouted Sidney, grabbing the frame and frantically trying to take out the photograph before it was ruined. "You absolute cow!"

"Whoops," said Lucinda, pressing her hand to her mouth theatrically. "Silly me."

"I'll pay you back for this," said Sidney, her hands shaking with fury as she pulled the damp photograph from its sodden frame and wiped it on her cardigan.

"You're going to be sorry you were ever born."

"Ooh, I'm *so* scared," said Lucinda with a mock shudder.

Sidney barged past her, knocking her shoulder, and marched out of the room, slamming the door behind her. She clattered down the stairs and along the out-of-bounds part of the corridor towards the garden. She couldn't face breakfast today. She needed to get outside.

As she passed the library where they had met the dowager countess, she recalled Lucinda's face when the dowager had told them about the Lady in Grey. Wouldn't it be wonderful to give Lucinda a proper fright? To watch her completely lose her dignity and run away screaming in terror.

She opened the door that led out to the terrace and paced round the side of the house to the South Lawn, fizzing with anger. She had never been there before. It was probably forbidden, but who cared?

The whole south front of the house was one enormous room with vast windows. It looked like one of the galleries in the British Museum, which her mother had dragged her round once. She'd nearly died of boredom.

The statues were swathed in dust sheets, presumably to protect them from bomb damage. With the figures all draped in white cloth, it looked like a gallery of ghosts.

An image popped into Sidney's head. An amazing image.

Was it possible? Oh, it would be extraordinary if

it could be done. But how could she make it happen?

When she reached the far side of the house, she turned round. The rooms in the East Wing were part of the school, and she might be seen through a window. She paced back beside the gallery, deep in thought. It was a marvellous idea, but she didn't see how she could pull it off. It needed another person, but it couldn't be Ginny or Phyllis, in case Lucinda guessed what was happening. And there was nobody else she could trust enough.

The photo was almost dry now, though the back of the frame was still sodden. The water had curled the paper and discoloured George's face, and the picture would never be the same. It was the only photo she had of him. She would have to ask him to have another one taken on his next leave.

It was a glorious day, and she was tempted to stay outdoors in the sunshine, but her fury-fuelled rebelliousness was beginning to wear off, and she couldn't bear to go through another deathly detention. She glanced at her wristwatch. If she hurried, she would just about make it to breakfast on time. She reluctantly went inside.

The library door was ajar and a newspaper lay open on the huge dining table. Sidney looked at it longingly. It was bound to say something about Dunkirk. Perhaps it would mention the role of the RAF and give her a clue as to why George hadn't been in touch. She hated that Lucinda's words had rattled her, but they really had.

Holding her breath, she slipped inside, closing

the door behind her. She walked over to the table and turned the newspaper to the front page. The headlines were all about Italy declaring war on Britain and France. Because of this there had been anti-Italian riots all over Britain. Italian ice-cream shops and restaurants had been smashed up in London, Liverpool and Edinburgh. It seemed very unfair, Sidney thought, to take things out on the poor ice-cream sellers.

Footsteps in the corridor. Stopping outside the door. Oh, help!

Sidney glanced wildly around the room and spotted an armchair in the far corner. She darted across and squeezed behind it, her heart thumping.

Was that a footstep on the floorboards? Whoever had come in was being extremely quiet. Sidney craned her neck to peep out.

It was that red-headed maid again, the one who somehow knew Shakespeare. She carried a housemaid's box but she was behaving very strangely. She tiptoed over to a writing desk on the other side of the room, glanced around furtively and then pulled the drawer open and looked inside.

Sidney stared. She hadn't had her down as the thieving type, but you never knew. They'd once had a parlourmaid who'd seemed terribly moral but had been caught taking wads of cash from her mother's purse.

Whatever the maid had been looking for, she didn't find it. She closed the drawer and walked over to the bookshelves.

Below the bookcases were little panelled cupboards with brass doorknobs. The maid crouched down, opened a cupboard and peered inside.

What a cheek, to steal from her employers! Especially when the poor old dowager seemed so fond of her.

Sidney stood up. "Well," she said. "Fancy meeting you here."

# CHAPTER SIXTEEN

# The Most Legendary Prank Ever

Nancy shot upright so fast she nearly fell backwards. She wheeled round to see one of the schoolgirls standing behind an armchair, where she'd obviously been hiding.

"What on earth are you doing?" the girl asked accusingly.

"I could ask you the same thing," said Nancy.

"Well, *I'm* not creeping about in my employer's library, searching in cupboards and drawers. It looks pretty fishy to me."

Nancy felt a coldness in the pit of her stomach. "What do you mean?"

The girl raised her eyebrows. "I'm just saying if I reported what I've seen to the butler, it wouldn't look terribly good, would it?"

"You wouldn't do that," Nancy said, hoping she sounded more confident than she felt. Oh why hadn't she been more careful and checked the room before she started searching? But what was the girl doing hiding behind a chair anyway?

The schoolgirl spread out her palms in a considering

gesture. "Perhaps it's my duty, as a guest in Lord Evesham's house, to report any underhand activities of his staff."

Nancy turned hot with anger. "How dare you threaten me!"

She took her dustpan and brush out of her box, walked over to the far side of the library and kneeled down to sweep the carpet.

The girl seemed to have a change of heart. "Listen, I don't really think you were stealing. But you were looking for something, weren't you? What were you looking for?"

"I need to get on with my work," said Nancy. She carried on sweeping, but the girl hovered close by, as if wanting to say something. Nancy took the comb out of the box and started on the fringe of the rug.

"Gosh, do you comb all the fringes?" said the girl. "It must take an absolute age."

Nancy ignored her.

"It must be rather fun being a housemaid," the girl said. "Wearing that sweet uniform. All that freedom and being properly grown-up."

Nancy stared at her. "Freedom? Fun? Cleaning from six in the morning until nine at night? Being shouted at by a foul-tempered cook and a snooty butler? Scrubbing lavatories, washing stone floors on hands and knees, brushing carpets, polishing furniture, cleaning windows?"

"But you're out in the world and earning your own money. That must be lovely."

"I'm earning money to support my family. My father was gassed in the last war and he's too ill to work most of the time."

"Oh, gosh, I'm sorry. Has he been to Switzerland?" Nancy gaped at her.

"One of my father's friends was gassed," said the girl, "and he spends a lot of time at a sanatorium in the Swiss Alps. The mountain air is meant to help. Your mother should arrange for your father to go. Mind you, it's probably terribly difficult to get there at the moment, with the war and everything."

Nancy was actually lost for words. Rich people really did live in a different world.

"I need to get on with my work," she said. "And don't you have to be somewhere?"

The girl glanced at her fancy wristwatch. "I've already missed breakfast. I'll say I went to Matron with a headache. I'll go to assembly, but it doesn't start for ten minutes."

Nancy went back to her work, but the girl still hung around awkwardly. Would she never leave?

Eventually she cleared her throat and said, "Actually, I need your help."

Ah, so that explained it. Of all the cheek!

"Listen," said the girl, "I want to get my own back on Lucinda, and I know you despise her as much as I do."

"Despise her? You've got a funny way of showing it. You look as thick as thieves to me."

"Well, it's complicated. She's in my dorm, and I like Ginny and Phyllis, so... But Lucinda's beastly.

She deliberately ruined my brother's picture this morning." She held out a discoloured photograph. "Lucinda poured water all over it because I told her she was vile and nobody liked her."

"That's RAF uniform, isn't it? Was your brother at Dunkirk?"

The girl's face grew tense. "I don't know. We haven't heard from him for a while."

Nancy felt a sympathy that took her by surprise. She knew how awful she would feel if she still hadn't heard from Jack.

"Anyway," said the girl, "I've thought of a way to pay Lucinda back. But I need somebody else, and it can't be anyone from school."

She started gabbling out some ridiculous plan involving the statues in the Long Gallery. Nancy stared at her in scorn. "We're about to be invaded by the Nazis and you're planning a prank on your schoolfriend?"

"She's not my friend. And she needs her comeuppance. So do say you'll help. It'll be fun."

"Fun! For you, maybe, but I'll lose my job."

"Only if we get caught. Which we won't. Besides, you don't like your job."

"It makes no difference whether I like it or not. My family needs the money. Not for a sanatorium in Switzerland, but for food and clothes and coal for the fire. And if I get sacked without a reference, I won't get another job. So I'd never risk my place here by stealing from my employer or by helping you with your stupid schemes."

The girl was silent for a moment. Then she looked directly into Nancy's eyes. Her expression had hardened.

"You might not have been stealing, but you were rifling through his lordship's drawers and cupboards. And if I went to his lordship's butler and told him that, how would you explain yourself?"

Nancy looked at her in disgust, but her heart was thumping in fear. "Are you blackmailing me?"

The girl shrugged. "All I'm saying is, if you want me to keep quiet about what you were doing in here, you need to do exactly what I'm about to tell you."

Nancy was silent. She loathed this girl with every fibre of her being, but she couldn't see any way out of the situation. "Fine," she said eventually. "But you'd better make sure I don't get caught."

The girl clapped her hands in glee. "I will, I promise. Oh, goody! This is going to be the most legendary prank ever. Right, I need to get to assembly, so let's quickly go through the details." She held out her hand. "I'm Sidney, by the way. And I know your name already."

"No, you don't. How?"

"I heard the dowager countess talking to you, the first day we were here. You're Margaret, aren't you?"

# CHAPTER SEVENTEEN

## The Dare

Miss Rutter took the Lower Fourth for Music Appreciation that afternoon. In order to keep the girls' hands as well as their minds healthily occupied, she had hit upon the idea of combining Music Appreciation with war work, so they were knitting socks for soldiers while listening to *The Pirates of Penzance*. They were supposed to work in silence, of course, but in the back row it was possible to murmur at a pitch that Miss Rutter couldn't hear above the music.

On reflection, Sidney did not feel at all proud of her behaviour towards Nancy, as she now knew her name to be. It wasn't terribly nice to use blackmail. But she couldn't afford to dwell on the rights and wrongs of the business. Lucinda had to be punished, and this would be the perfect way of doing it. She just needed to introduce her plan in a way that seemed natural.

"Look," whispered Phyllis, nudging Sidney and looking out of the window. The dowager countess, with her lady's maid supporting her arm, was walking hesitantly across the lawn.

This was her chance.

"I wonder if the dowager has seen the ghost of the Lady in Grey recently," Sidney said.

"She didn't say she'd ever seen it, did she?" said Phyllis.

"I'm sure she has," said Sidney. "She said she communes with spirits, didn't she?"

"I don't believe in ghosts," said Ginny.

"Nobody does," said Sidney, "until they see one."

"Oh, shut up, new girl," said Lucinda.

Sidney continued to knit, a warm glow of pleasure suffusing her as she pictured Lucinda's imminent downfall. "I heard another story about the Lady in Grey last week," she said casually.

"What story?" asked Phyllis.

"It's very sad."

"Who told it to you?" asked Ginny.

"The gardener's boy. When I was planting lettuces."

Lucinda gave a dismissive laugh. "You're listening to peasants' tales now, are you?"

"It's all true. Albert's family have worked on the estate for hundreds of years. They know everything about the place."

"They make it up, you mean," said Lucinda. "That's what servants do. You can't believe anything they say. Surely your parents taught you that at least?"

"I didn't believe it either," said Sidney, "but Albert swore it was in a book somewhere, so I sneaked into the library at morning break and found it. It's an old leather-bound book with gold edges, called *A Complete History of Stanbrook House.*"

Lucinda said nothing, but she was clearly curious. Sidney knew it was important to make the details believable. So far, so good.

"So what's the story?" asked Ginny.

"I can't tell you. You'd be too frightened."

"Frightened!" scoffed Lucinda.

Miss Rutter looked up from her marking with a frown. "Silence, girls."

They bent over their socks and knitted diligently until the music reached a loud part. Miss Rutter was busy scribbling on another unfortunate essay.

"Tell us," whispered Ginny.

Sidney looked slowly along the row at each of them in turn. "I'll tell you if you'll accept a dare."

Ginny's eyes lit up. "Go on."

"All right. I dare you all to come to the Long Gallery with me at midnight. I'll tell you the story there."

"Why the Long Gallery?" asked Phyllis.

"Because that's where it happened."

Lucinda sniffed. "That's a pathetic dare."

Sidney raised her eyebrows and resumed her knitting. "Sounds as though somebody's scared."

"Of course I'm not scared," hissed Lucinda. "But the Long Gallery's out of bounds. We'd all be expelled if we were caught."

"Isn't that the point of a dare? That it's dangerous? But I understand if you're too frightened to accept."

"I'm not frightened. It's just so pathetic it's not worth accepting. Walking to the Long Gallery while you tell a stupid story? What sort of dare is that?"

"All right," said Sidney. "I bet you two shillings that by the end of the story you will run from the Long Gallery screaming in terror."

She didn't actually have two shillings, but that didn't worry her. She was a hundred per cent sure that the next morning she would be two shillings richer.

"My father says only common people bet," said Lucinda.

"I'll take your bet," said Ginny. "I never scream, and I'd like the two shillings."

"Super," said Sidney. "Tonight then. I'll set my alarm for eleven thirty."

# CHAPTER EIGHTEEN

## On the Stroke of Midnight

The four girls tiptoed out of the dormitory in their dressing gowns and slippers. It wasn't completely dark, thank goodness – a dim lamp was left on all night in the corridor.

*Creeeaak.* Phyllis stepped on a loose floorboard.

They froze. Lucinda shot her a poisonous look. But nobody stirred behind the closed doors.

Screwing up her face in terror, Phyllis eased her foot off the loose board. They breathed again.

They tiptoed down the two long flights of stairs to the ground floor, then across the marble tiles of the hall, past the grandfather clock with its steady tick-tock heartbeat.

A notice hung on the door of the Long Gallery, written on cardboard in Miss Hathersage's neat capital letters.

**STRICTLY OUT OF BOUNDS TO PUPILS.**

Sidney turned the handle and led the others in. The gallery wasn't blacked out. There was no need, since nobody ever went in there at night. Moonlight shone through the high French windows, casting a ghostly glow on the shrouded statues. The draped sculpture of Cupid in front of the central window looked slightly bulkier than the others, but was that just her imagination? What if Nancy hadn't shown up? Sidney had suggested that she made a little spy hole in the sheet, but she couldn't see any holes from here.

Phyllis shivered. "I don't like this. It's too spooky."

"Oh, grow up, baby," snapped Lucinda. But she sounded nervy. Good.

"So," Sidney said, "you've all heard about the second Countess of Stanbrook, whose ghost is said to haunt the house in the form of a Lady in Grey." She spoke in a low voice, leading them towards the centre of the gallery. She stopped a few yards in front of Cupid's statue, so that she had her back to the statue and the others were facing it.

"You've heard how she's said to walk the ramparts and wander in the Italian Garden, night after night, wailing and wringing her hands, desperately searching for the husband who abandoned her."

"Yes, we know," said Lucinda. "I hope you haven't brought us down here just to tell us that again."

"Of course not. I've found out something else about her ghost. Something the dowager countess didn't tell us. Something that happens in this very room."

Phyllis was wide-eyed. "What is it?"

"After the countess died, the earl, filled with remorse for ruining her life, had a marble statue made of her, and placed it in this very gallery. There's a photograph of it in the book in the library. It's beautiful."

Phyllis glanced around at the white-sheeted figures. "Which one is it?"

"I don't know. We've never seen them uncovered, have we?"

"So what happens in this room?" asked Ginny.

"Well, the book says that one summer night, on the stroke of midnight, in this very room, the earl finally confessed to his wife that he was in love with another woman. He left her here, and she went mad with grief. Every night, she wandered the house and grounds, weeping and wailing and wringing her hands. And every night at midnight she returned to this gallery, pacing and pacing, hoping against hope that tonight her husband would return and tell her it was all a terrible mistake and she was his one true love. But he never did."

Sidney lowered her voice to a whisper. "And every year, on the anniversary of the night on which her heart was broken, the barriers crumble between the worlds of the living and the dead, and her unquiet spirit returns to haunt this place. And on the stroke of midnight, the statue of the Lady in Grey comes to life."

Phyllis shrieked, which made Ginny and Lucinda jump. The sound echoed around the gallery. Lucinda, her face deathly white, glared at Phyllis, who clapped her hand over her mouth.

Sidney waited until she had their full attention

again. "On the stroke of midnight," she whispered, "her solid-marble statue transforms to flesh and bone. And this pitiful vision of shrivelled flesh, on its antique skeleton, steps down from its plinth and goes in search of an innocent young girl on whom to take its revenge."

She paused. All three of them were transfixed. Lucinda was gripping Ginny's arm, while her eyes flitted in terror from one shrouded statue to another.

"It wanders the Long Gallery," Sidney continued, "searching for the scent of a young girl's blood. And when it finds its victim, its skeletal white fingers reach out and grip her pure young shoulders, and its skeletal jaw rattles open, and it sinks its skeletal teeth into the girl's shoulder." Sidney made her voice as low as it could go, and spoke the next words very, very slowly. "And it sucks out her blood."

Phyllis whimpered.

Sidney had prepared a lot more detail about the victim's blood being slowly drained from her weakening body, and she was prepared to draw it out for several more minutes if necessary. But as she began her next sentence she heard the sound she'd been waiting for: the whirring of the grandfather clock as it prepared to strike.

The first stroke of midnight sounded from the hall. Lucinda gasped and gripped Ginny's arm even harder. Ginny looked pale and tense. Phyllis clung to Ginny. And then, with a rustle of fabric, and a low groaning sound, the shrouded statue in front of them appeared to shift and sway into life.

# CHAPTER NINETEEN

## Frozen in Terror

For a split second they stood stock-still, petrified. Then Lucinda and Ginny started screaming hysterically. Phyllis slid down Ginny's side and crumpled to the ground.

Sidney turned, saw the movements under the dust sheet and joined in the hysteria with a high-pitched scream. But her mind was working frantically. She needed to get the others away so Nancy could flee before anybody came to investigate.

Ginny slapped Phyllis's face. "Get up!" she yelled. "She's coming for us!"

Phyllis moaned and shakily got up.

Lucinda was running for the door, sobbing. Sidney grabbed Phyllis's hand.

"Run!" Sidney cried. "Help me, Ginny!"

Ginny grabbed Phyllis's other hand and they pulled her to the door. Lucinda was fumbling with the doorknob, sobbing and gasping.

Sidney shook her by the shoulders. "Be quiet! Or we'll get caught!"

Lucinda swung round, her face wild with fury, and

shoved Sidney back. "Get away from me!"

Sidney stumbled and fell. Scrambling to her feet, she realised that in this state Lucinda didn't care in the slightest for the wrath of the teachers. The only thing she cared about was getting away from the skeletal ghost that wanted to suck her blood.

With a violent wrench of the handle, Lucinda pulled the door open and staggered into the hall. Ginny and Phyllis ran out after her, weeping and wailing.

"Ssh," hissed Sidney desperately as they lurched towards the stairs. "You'll wake the teachers. We're safe out here. She can't leave the gallery. It said so in the story."

The others blundered blindly up the staircase behind Lucinda, still sobbing. Sidney raced after them, overtaking Phyllis and Ginny. She had to stop them. "Aargh!" she moaned, grabbing Lucinda's arm.

"Get off me!" spat Lucinda. "What are you doing?"

Sidney sank down on the stair, keeping her grip on Lucinda's arm and clutching her ankle with her other hand, blocking the way for Ginny and Phyllis. "I've sprained my ankle. I can't move."

"Don't be stupid," said Lucinda, casting a fearful glance down the staircase. "Get up!"

"Shut up!" hissed Sidney. "We're safe now. I told you: she only haunts the gallery. But if you lot carry on screaming, you'll wake the whole school and we'll be expelled. Do you understand?"

This seemed to finally get through to them. They quietened their hysterics to choked sobs and hiccups.

"I want to go to bed," wept Lucinda.

"Go," said Sidney. "I'll limp up behind you."

Lucinda didn't wait to be told twice. She stumbled on up the stairs. Ginny and Phyllis stepped over Sidney and followed her.

"Will you be all right?" asked Ginny, glancing back.

Sidney stood up. "Yes, I'll hobble up. You go on, don't worry."

Her latest letter to George was sticking out of her dressing-gown pocket, where she had put it for safekeeping after finishing it by torchlight under the bedclothes. She tucked it back into her pocket. Then she turned ice-cold.

She had put her pen in the pocket too. Her fountain pen with her name engraved on it. And now it wasn't there.

She frantically felt in her other pocket, but it was empty except for her torch. She took it out and shone the feeble bulb across the stair. Nothing. She would have to retrace her steps.

With a lurch in her stomach, she realised exactly when the pen had fallen out of her pocket. It must have been when Lucinda had pushed her over in the gallery. She crept downstairs, scanning each stair with the torch, but there was no sign of it.

The door to the gallery was still open. Nancy was tiptoeing across the room, her head down. Sidney slipped inside and closed the door behind her.

Nancy jumped in shock. Then she saw Sidney and scowled. "What are you doing?"

"I dropped my pen," said Sidney, sweeping her torch beam around the floor. "It's got my name engraved on it, so I couldn't risk— Oh, here it is!" She swooped on the pen, which had rolled to the base of a plinth, and put it back in her pocket. "Thank goodness!"

"Right, I'm getting out of here," said Nancy. "I hope you're satisfied with your little prank."

"It was marvellous. Better than I could have dreamed. They were utterly petrified, weren't they? Did you see—"

But Nancy had turned rigid, and the colour had drained from her flushed cheeks.

Sidney listened. Voices and footsteps, coming towards the doors.

They stared at each other, frozen in terror.

Sidney's legs trembled. "Hide!" she whispered. "Under the dust sheet! I'll go here."

She ducked under the nearest sheet and scrambled on to the plinth, just as Nancy disappeared back under Cupid's sheet. Sidney stood up and hastily adjusted the fabric so it covered her completely. She leaned against the cold hard marble, her heart thumping.

Who would come to the Long Gallery at this time of night? And why?

# CHAPTER TWENTY

## Interesting Developments

Sidney heard the door at the other end of the gallery open and close again. Footsteps echoed on the marble floor, and the smell of cigar smoke drifted through the air.

She noticed a little rip in the dust sheet, just to the side of her right eye.

As the footsteps drew closer, she shifted the sheet very, very slowly, until she could see through the hole.

Two people, both holding half-smoked cigars, stopped a few feet in front of Cupid. Sidney's heartbeat sped up. It was Lord Evesham and the blonde-haired woman who'd been with him in the gardens and, she was pretty sure, in the stable yard at midnight.

"Sorry to drag you away from the brandy," said Lord Evesham in a low voice. "Safer to talk in here, without servants in and out all the time."

Sidney held her breath. Now she would find out what was really going on.

"You're not concerned, are you, Gerald?" said

the woman. "You don't think anybody's been planted here?"

"No, no, absolutely not. We can't be too careful, that's all."

"You said there had been interesting developments?"

"I met Lonsdale again yesterday," said Lord Evesham. "He gave an excellent report of the progress being made in Whitehall. We have members working in every government department. Even in the War Cabinet."

"That's terrific news, Gerald."

"He says the main body of the police is with us too. There's a bad patch up above, including our local chief constable, who's a staunch supporter of Churchill unfortunately. But we're not without help, even at the top."

Sidney frowned. Why was it bad to support Churchill? That didn't make sense.

"And what about the forces?" asked the woman. "Have you made progress there?"

"I was coming to that," said Lord Evesham. "It's excellent news."

"Go on."

"Obviously this mustn't be written down, nor a word breathed outside this room, but we have every reason to believe that General Steel will join us when the time comes."

The woman's eyebrows shot up. "Steel? Really?"

"He won't come out into the open until the moment arrives, of course. Far too risky – he's essentially the head of the armed forces, after all. But we know from another general, who is one of us, that Steel admires fascism, and that he looks favourably on the prospect of a revolutionary fascist dictatorship in Britain."

*What?!*

Sidney gripped the statue, her heart thumping. A fascist dictatorship in Britain? And Lord Evesham supported that? No, she must have got it wrong.

"Well, that is excellent news," said the woman, flushed with excitement. "Hitler is a god. The energy he's given to the German people, the wonderful sense of purpose, the vision of a pure and prosperous nation... It changed my life, visiting Germany and seeing what he's achieved there. The thought of putting his ideals into practice over here is just too exciting for words."

Sidney turned as cold and still as the statue she clung to.

"Quite," said Lord Evesham. "Our system of government is rotten to the core. A bloody revolution is exactly what we need. With members in the Local Defence Volunteers ready to sabotage communications lines, and our members in the forces, defences will be thoroughly disrupted. The battle will be over very quickly."

"The glory of it!" said the woman. "Nazi flags all along the Mall. Hitler taking the victory salute from the balcony of Buckingham Palace. The joy of it all!"

"Obviously Hitler needs to destroy the Air

Force before the invasion can take place," said Lord Evesham.

The hairs on Sidney's arms rose and she felt suddenly faint. She leaned heavily against the statue.

"Absolutely," said the woman eagerly. "I'd love to undertake another mission."

"That won't be necessary," he said. "You did an excellent job at the Spitfire plant, but it's far safer and more efficient to let the Luftwaffe do it."

*She* had bombed the Spitfire factory? Sidney's palms turned clammy.

"I've managed to obtain the plans of every airfield and aircraft factory in the country," Lord Evesham said. "I'll hand them to the Germans next Friday in Ireland, and they'll be able to wipe out the RAF before they know what's hit them. France is bound to have surrendered by then, and the Führer can focus his full attention here."

*Wipe out the RAF!* Sidney's legs shook with rage and fear, and her palms were sweating so much that she was losing her grip on the marble.

"And are the pamphlets ready?" asked the woman.

"I've printed several thousand," he replied, "but we'll need a lot more. The difficulty is obtaining the paper, but I've found a reliable source now."

"Good," said the woman. "It will be vital to give the right information to the public immediately, otherwise all sorts of false rumours will start circulating."

"Quite," said Lord Evesham. "The pamphlets are the key to ensuring a smooth transition. Once we distribute them, the public will understand how Nazism will benefit them, and I have no doubt they'll embrace it very quickly."

"I've a plane I can borrow to do the leaflet drops over the northern cities," the woman said. "You can cover the south. But we'll need many more thousands of pamphlets."

"There'll be plenty," said Lord Evesham. "But I can only do a print run in the dead of night, and I have to be extremely careful. It would be death to the organisation if it were discovered."

"I can do some printing on nights when you're otherwise engaged," said the woman. "The machine won't give me any trouble."

"Better not," said Lord Evesham. "It has to be done in the utmost secrecy. Too much of a risk to have you involved."

"I'll make sure nobody gets wind of it. I was wondering if I could join you in Ireland too. I'd love to be there."

"And I'd love you to come, but you know the Germans – not keen on women in politics. Shall we head back to the library? I could do with another brandy."

"Before we go, Gerald," said the woman, "I wanted to let you know I'm drawing up a list of prominent opponents to Nazism. People who'll be strung up from lamp posts once the country's in our hands. Any names you have of anti-Nazis who can be added to the list would be much appreciated."

"Of course," said Lord Evesham.

"And there was one other thing I thought I should mention."

"Yes?" He sounded distracted, as though his mind was on the brandy.

"Obviously one of the first tasks of the new government will be to put race laws in place. It's vital to weed out Jewish influence in our institutions and public life."

"Indeed."

"And I imagine that, as prime minister, you would wish to use Stanbrook as the country headquarters of the new regime. I'm sure the Führer would be delighted with it."

"Undoubtedly."

"So you'd wish to set the right example and weed out any undesirable elements in your own household? It's vital that the aristocracy takes the lead in these things."

"Do you have a point to make, Dorothy?"

"Well, let's say I was rather shocked to discover that you have a Jewess working on the premises."

"What?" said Lord Evesham. "Absolute nonsense."

"I'm afraid not, Gerald. I spotted a housemaid on the lawn last week and I made a few discreet enquiries."

"Housemaid? I've never set eyes on the housemaids. My mother deals with the females. Although she's certainly let things slip recently. And it would be just like her to employ a Jewess, especially if she had a sob story. Don't worry. I'll get it seen to."

"And there was a boy working in the garden with only one arm."

"Oh, Albert? Family's worked here for generations. Lost it in a machine accident."

"Hmm. Still, one can't be too careful. It's vital to give the right impression." She gave a delicate cough. "And your mother, Gerald? I hear she's…"

"Yes?" There was a note of impatience in his voice.

"I hear she's rather deteriorated lately. In her mind. I know of a couple of places that might be suitable. I can send you the details. After all, you'll want her to be properly looked after. By specialists."

"Absolutely," said Lord Evesham. "I'll see to it. Just let me get this blasted dinner over with first."

"What dinner?"

"Oh, all the usual county bores are descending here next Thursday. Lord-lieutenant, high sheriff, chief constable, et cetera, et cetera. Some of them were friends of my father, and they're keen to pay their respects to my mother – fond of her for some reason. She won't be at the dinner, of course, but they'll want to see her beforehand. I'll keep it brief – she's really not fit to be out in public, but I think it's best that she continues to live here until then. Reassure them that nothing's going to change."

The woman raised her eyebrows. "Well, they're going to be in for quite a shock."

# CHAPTER TWENTY-ONE

# We've Got To Do Something

As the door closed behind them, Nancy clung to the statue, trembling with shock and rage. She had worshipped Dorothy Taylor her whole life. And she was a murderous fascist.

"Nancy!" hissed Sidney.

There was a swooshing of fabric, followed by a thud.

Nancy's legs shook as she climbed down from the plinth and emerged from under the sheet. Sidney was pale and wide-eyed with rage.

"Can you *believe* that?" she cried, tears in her eyes. "The lying, vicious, scheming *traitor*! Plotting to destroy the Air Force and help Hitler invade!"

"Shh," said Nancy urgently.

"Don't tell me to shush!" Sidney sobbed. "Didn't you hear what they said? They're planning to kill my brother! Don't you even care?"

"Of course I care," hissed Nancy, "but you don't want them to catch us, do you?" A shiver ran through her as she remembered Dorothy Taylor's words. "They've bombed the Spitfire factory. They want people strung up from lamp posts. Can you imagine what they'd do to us if they knew we'd heard all that?"

"We have to report them," said Sidney. "Before he can fly to Ireland and give those plans to the Nazis. We must go to the police first thing tomorrow."

"I've already done that," said Nancy.

Sidney stared at her. "What?"

"I overheard some things last week. He was talking to a man about going to Ireland on the twenty-first and personally handing things over to the Germans. He didn't say what he was handing over, but it sounded suspicious, so I reported it to Mr Armitage, and he said that his lordship is dealing with matters that common people like me can't possibly understand."

"But this is different!" cried Sidney.

"Shh! Keep your voice down."

"This is different," whispered Sidney. "We know exactly what he's planning now."

"Yes, and we have to stop him. That's why I was searching the library – looking for evidence. But I haven't found any. So it's our word against his, and guess who the police will believe? A schoolgirl and a housemaid, or a war-hero earl and a world-famous racing driver?"

"A what?"

"That woman is Dorothy Taylor. You must have heard of her."

Sidney shook her head.

"She's the top female racing-car driver in

the world."

"But surely the police will believe us if we both tell them what we heard," said Sidney. "I mean, why would we lie?"

Nancy gave a bitter laugh. "Well, they assumed I was playing a prank, and Mr Armitage thought I'd been turned hysterical by reading *Jane Eyre*."

Sidney frowned in confusion. "*Jane Eyre?*"

"Doesn't matter. The point is, they won't believe me. But maybe," she said, a glimmer of hope flickering inside her, "maybe they'll believe you, with your posh voice and your rich parents. You could tell your headmistress, and *she* could go to the police."

Sidney looked energised for a second, and then her shoulders slumped and her face clouded over. "No. Miss Hathersage worships the ground Lord Evesham walks on. And I've already been told off for having the wrong sort of imagination. There's no way she'd believe my word against Lord Evesham's."

Nancy shrugged. "There you are then."

"But we've got to do something!" Sidney said. "Or he'll hand over those plans and George will be killed!"

"And they'll round up all the Jews, like Rosa and her family," said Nancy, "and people like Albert, who don't look the way they want everyone to look, and poor old people like the dowager, just because they're a bit confused, and everyone who's said anything against the Nazis, and they'll put them in camps, and who knows what they'll do to them."

"Who's Rosa?" asked Sidney.

"The other housemaid. She—"

Sidney froze and put a finger to her lips.

"What?" said Nancy.

"I thought I heard a door shutting," Sidney whispered. "Get under the sheet."

Nancy scrabbled back on to the plinth, feeling sick with terror. She heard a faint murmur of voices in the distance, and then the sound of another door closing. She waited, ears strained for any more sounds, but the house stayed silent. After several minutes, she climbed down again.

"This isn't safe," she said, as Sidney appeared from her plinth. "We should meet in the morning and work out what to do. When can you meet?"

"They might not notice if I skip assembly," Sidney said. "Can you do eight forty-five?"

Nancy nodded. "There's a housemaid's closet on the first floor, just to the right of the main staircase. Meet me in there."

They crept up the back stairs in silence. It was strange to think of them working together, Nancy thought, when an hour ago she had loathed this girl. But the only thing that mattered now was to have Lord Evesham arrested. It was already the twelfth of June, and on the twenty-first he was planning to fly to Ireland and hand over the plans of every airfield and aircraft factory in Britain. And it was obvious that Sidney was as determined to stop him as she was. After all, her brother's life was at stake.

On the second-floor landing, Sidney headed to

her dormitory, and Nancy continued up to the attic. She lay awake for hours before she finally fell into a troubled, restless doze. When her alarm rang at six, she woke with a pounding heart, and the previous night's events flooded back into her head.

This time one fact surfaced above all the other horrors. Rosa was going to be sacked.

Where would she go? She wouldn't be able to stay with her parents in their employer's attic.

Suddenly Nancy had an idea. She got out of bed and took her writing paper from the drawer.

When she met Rosa at the housemaids' closet, she handed her a sealed envelope. It was addressed but not stamped.

"That's my parents' address," she said. "Keep this letter on you." She took Rosa's hand and looked into her eyes. "Rosa, things are getting dangerous. If anything happens, promise me you'll go to my parents and give them this letter."

Rosa turned pale. "Are you in trouble? Tell me."

Nancy shook her head. "Don't worry about me; I'm absolutely fine. I can't say any more, but if anything happens to you, take this to my parents and stay there while they read it. Promise?"

Rosa's face was tense and terrified. "I promise," she said.

# CHAPTER TWENTY-TWO

## Summoned by the Sage

When Sidney was jolted awake by the clang of the rising bell, she felt as though she'd only just gone to sleep. She had lain awake for hours, her heart beating very fast, snatches of that disturbing conversation swimming through her head.

Oh, *please* let there be a letter from George today.

Ginny's bedsprings creaked as she shifted on to her side. Sidney slipped out of bed. If she could dress and head to the bathroom before the others got up, she could hopefully avoid any conversation.

"You came back eventually then," mumbled Ginny.

"Mm," said Sidney, pulling on her stockings.

"Took your time. Is your ankle all right?"

"Not too bad. A bit painful." Sidney made a mental note to remember to limp.

More creaking of bedsprings. "I can't get up," moaned Phyllis. "I feel like death."

"Stop whining," came Lucinda's muffled voice. "You were such a baby last night."

"*Me?!*" squeaked Phyllis, sitting bolt upright

in indignation.

"I was playing along," said Lucinda. "Just for fun. There wasn't anything there really."

"But you saw and heard it. We all did."

"It was just your imagination playing tricks. Shadows and the wind. I wasn't really scared."

Sidney took her blouse from the bedside chair.

"It was real," said Phyllis. "Wasn't it, Ginny?"

"There was certainly *something* under that dust sheet," said Ginny. "Whether it was a ghost or not, though... I'd be very interested to hear what you think, Sidney."

Sidney's stomach clenched. She buttoned up her blouse and kept her head down as she crossed the room with her wash bag.

"I think you owe me two shillings," she said.

Miss Hathersage never came to breakfast in the dining hall. The girls were certain that she feasted on eggs and bacon in her room, while they had to force down disgusting lumpy porridge.

Miss Rutter was in charge, and before anybody was allowed to eat there were Breakfast Notices. Today was the usual list of order marks, merit points, crimes and misdemeanours.

"And finally," said Miss Rutter, "Sidney Dashworth is to report to Miss Hathersage's study immediately after breakfast."

The hairs on Sidney's arms stood up. A creeping coldness crawled along her limbs. How had Miss Hathersage found out? Had somebody seen her tiptoeing back to the dorm? Had she left some incriminating evidence?

Phyllis, Ginny and Lucinda stared at her, rigid with fear.

"Why have you been summoned by the Sage?" asked Amanda.

Sidney shrugged. "Who knows? Probably for running naked across the lawns again."

Jean opened her eyes wide and Phyllis giggled nervously. Lucinda gave Sidney a fierce warning look and Sidney shot a scornful glance back. As if she would snitch.

The walk to the headmistress's study took forever. How was she going to explain her midnight ramblings? Sneaking down to take food from the kitchens? That would probably get her expelled, but she was bound to be expelled anyway. The crucial thing was to convince the headmistress she'd acted alone, so the others wouldn't get in trouble.

As she passed an open classroom door, her eye was caught by a movement at the window. It was a beautiful peacock butterfly, beating its wings frantically against the glass.

"Oh, you poor thing," said Sidney, hurrying into the room. "Don't worry, I'll set you free."

She fumbled with the catch and flung the window open.

"There," she said. "Have a lovely summer. I'm so glad you don't just live for a day."

The butterfly flew out and fluttered across the garden, landing on a perfect white rose. Sidney gazed at the big round eyes on its wing tips. They looked like the circles painted on RAF planes, she thought.

Her stomach was in knots as she knocked on the headmistress's door.

"Enter."

Miss Hathersage was standing at the window, looking out across the gardens. When Sidney came in, she glanced at her and indicated the chair opposite her desk. "Sit down, Sidney."

Sidney sat. Miss Hathersage walked back to her desk and sat down too. She caught Sidney's eye, then bowed her head and clasped her hands. She took a deep breath and said, "Sidney, I am afraid I have some bad news for you. You must be brave and bear it as well as you can."

*George.*

Waves of heat and cold pulsated through her body. Heavy, weightless, heavy, weightless.

"Your father telephoned me this morning to say that he and your mother had received a telegram. I am afraid your brother's plane has been shot down in France."

Sidney jumped to her feet. "But that doesn't mean... He could have escaped. He would have ejected. He might be a prisoner of war."

"I'm afraid not, Sidney."

"How do you know? How can you know?" cried Sidney wildly.

"I am afraid the telegram said 'Missing believed killed'."

Sidney's legs felt cold and wobbly. She dropped

back into the chair.

"I'm so sorry, Sidney. I hope it will give you some comfort to remember that your brother died heroically, fighting for freedom against a terrible tyranny. His sacrifice was for a noble cause."

Sidney closed her eyes and clamped her hands over her ears.

She heard the sound of a drawer opening.

"Take this," said Miss Hathersage.

She opened her eyes to see the headmistress handing her a banknote.

"Your mother would like you to go home for a few days. I said I would lend you the money for the train fare. Pack your overnight bag and catch the bus to the station. There is a bus stop at the end of the drive. You will be in plenty of time to catch the eleven twenty train, and your mother is arranging for your aunt to meet you at Paddington and see you across London." She stood up. "Strength, Sidney. Your mother will need you to show strength and courage. It is at times like this that we show what we are truly made of. This is your chance to help your country and honour your brother."

Numbly Sidney stood up and took the money. She stumbled out of the room and walked down the corridor. As she reached the staircase, she stopped. Her mind was a howling blizzard in a blinding white fog. Impossible to slow the whirling flakes and settle them into thoughts. What was she meant to do? Pack a bag, Miss Hathersage had said. But what would she put in it?

Impossible to walk upstairs. Her legs were too wobbly and weak.

Station. Home.

Which way? Where was the door? Door.

She turned and stumbled back down the corridor towards the light at the far end. She fumbled with the handle. Why wouldn't the door open? Open!

Then it opened and she was plunged outside into the blinding sun. Why was the sun shining? How could the sun shine?

Where was she supposed to go?

Home. Bus.

She stumbled numbly towards the drive.

"Hey!"

Footsteps. Maid stepping in front of her. Angry maid with laundry basket. Nancy.

"Where are you going?" Nancy asked.

Sidney stared past her blankly.

"We were meant to meet fifteen minutes ago, remember?" said Nancy. "Where do you think you're going?"

Words. Words. Nothing.

Sidney stumbled past her.

Bus. Home.

"Hey, don't you dare ignore me!" called Nancy. "What do you think you're playing at? I thought you cared about this. You said you'd help!"

Bus. Bus to station.

Footsteps behind her.

"You selfish little coward," hissed Nancy. "I suppose you've had a letter saying your brother's fine, and now you think nothing else matters. But how will you feel when we're invaded and you have to live under the Nazis? I suppose you think it won't affect you in your privileged little bubble. But it will, you know. It will affect all of us. And you still refuse to stand up against it. You're no better than a traitor yourself, you selfish, cowardly thing."

Bus. Home. Train. Home. With the words repeating over and over in her head, Sidney stumbled on down the drive.

# CHAPTER TWENTY-THREE

## We'll Never
## Tell a Soul

Nancy stomped back to the house, fuming. After all she'd done for that spoilt little brat, spending hours standing under a dust sheet, almost falling asleep on her feet after working all day, just for a stupid prank. And then to be betrayed like that. Oh yes, Sidney had said all those high-minded things last night, but when it actually came down to it, what had she done? Run away, without even a word of apology.

*Serves you right, Nancy*, she told herself. *That'll teach you to trust a rich girl. All they care about in the end is themselves and their rich friends. You're just going to have to keep searching for evidence on your own, same as you were doing before.*

Suddenly a thought struck her with such force that she gasped. Lord Evesham had a printing press! He was printing pamphlets to drop from planes! Pamphlets to explain why a Nazi government was a good thing.

That was *exactly* the evidence she needed. If she could find those pamphlets, then people would have to believe that Lord Evesham supported the Nazis.

"Ah, Nancy," said Mr Armitage, as she came into the servants' hall. "Mr Burford is taking Miss Morris to Oxford this morning to buy dressmaking materials for her ladyship. Miss Morris has suggested that you stay with her ladyship until she returns. She says her ladyship enjoys your company."

He sounded surprised, but Nancy chose not to take offence. It would be a pleasure to spend the morning with the dowager. Even cleaning her rooms was a pleasure compared with cleaning Lord Evesham's. His apartment was dark and cluttered, and stank of cigarette smoke, but hers was light and airy, filled with pretty ornaments and interesting mementoes of her happy childhood.

Nancy's insides flipped as she remembered Dorothy Taylor's words last night. What a cruel suggestion, to take the old lady away from her home and the people who cared for her.

The dowager was an early riser, and she would often come and sit in the drawing room while Nancy was working. Sometimes she would be wearing her elegant silk dressing gown, and sometimes she was already beautifully dressed and coiffed. Much to Miss Morris's disapproval, the dowager liked to interrupt Nancy in her work.

"Do stop that beastly dusting, my dear. Come over here and rest your poor feet. Hilda, bring me my shell collection."

She would pat the sofa beside her and ask Nancy to sit down, while Miss Morris, with pursed lips, would fetch the carved wooden box. The dowager would open it and, with a rapt and faraway expression on her face, take out the beautiful seashells and tell Nancy all about her long-ago holidays on the Isle of Wight. Sometimes she would ask Miss Morris to fetch her album of pressed wild flowers, each one neatly labelled, and she would tell stories of her rambles with Margaret.

Nancy never quite knew what to expect from these conversations. Sometimes the countess would simply say, "How you remind me of Margaret, my dear. The resemblance is simply uncanny." At other times, though, the dowager really seemed to think that Nancy was her childhood friend, and would talk to her as though they were still young girls.

Nancy knocked at the apartment door. She heard Miss Morris pad across the room and turn the key in the lock.

"Her ladyship had a bad night's sleep," said Miss Morris, when she opened the door.

When Miss Morris said this, it generally meant that Nancy was about to spend the morning being Margaret. The lady's maid looked exhausted, and it occurred to Nancy for the first time that if the dowager had had a bad night, Miss Morris had probably had a bad night too.

Although the dowager was immaculately turned out as usual, she looked distracted and far away. As soon as Miss Morris left for Oxford, she whispered to Nancy, "I'm glad she's gone, my dear. Aren't you?"

Nancy smiled.

"I don't trust her, Margaret," said the dowager.

"I think she's the one who sneaked on us when we took the cake from the pantry."

"Oh," said Nancy. "Yes."

"I saw him last night, you know," said the dowager.

Nancy glanced at her. Her tone had changed. With Miss Morris absent, Nancy felt bold enough to ask a question.

"Who did you see, my lady?"

"Why, Edward, of course. At the foot of my bed."

"Oh." Edward was her late husband.

"He warned me," the dowager continued. "Told me not to trust Gerald. He's up to something, he said. Got in with the wrong crowd up at Oxford. They're a bad lot, he said. No good will come of it. Not like his brother. He knew right from wrong. But Gerald was always difficult. I should have been more firm with him. I never knew what to do with him."

Nancy turned hot and then cold. Did she dare ask questions, or would that make the dowager remember she was talking to a housemaid?

She took a deep breath. "What is he up to?"

The dowager didn't seem to hear her. "Not like Richard. Such a good boy. So kind and thoughtful. Do you remember the time he rescued the injured fox, Margaret?" And Nancy listened to her memories of her eldest son, now buried in an unknown French field.

When Nancy went to clean the dressing room, the dowager followed her, sitting in the little armchair while Nancy dusted the dressing table and the mantelpiece. She was dusting family photographs

142

when the old lady suddenly got up and walked to the wardrobe. To Nancy's alarm, the dowager gripped the edge of the heavy wardrobe with her thin frail hands and tried to pull it away from the oak-panelled wall.

"Don't do that, your ladyship," she said, hurrying to the wardrobe and bracing herself against it, though the dowager would never be able to move the enormous piece of furniture. "Why don't you sit down? If you need to reach something, ask me and I'll do it."

But the dowager kept tugging at the wardrobe. "Oh, I told him not to put it there!" she exclaimed. "I told him and he wouldn't listen!"

"If you sit down, my lady, I can ring for somebody to help me move it."

The dowager threw her hands up in despair. "Oh, why has he put it there? I begged him not to, but he said I was being silly."

She flopped down in the armchair, pressed her hands over her face and broke into violent sobs.

"My lady," said Nancy, dashing to the chair and putting her arm round the dowager, shocked to feel how thin she was, "what's the matter?"

The dowager raised her head and gave Nancy an extraordinarily intense gaze. Her eyes were startlingly blue. "How will we get in now?"

"How will we get in where, your ladyship?"

"Why, the secret passage, of course!"

Nancy stared at her. "Secret passage? Behind the wardrobe?"

"Do you remember the day we found it, my dear? We must have pressed every panel in the house in our search."

Nancy felt her heart beating faster. Was there really a secret passage? Where did it lead? Or was the dowager just imagining it?

The old lady seemed about to drift off, but Nancy needed to hear more. "You must have been so excited when you found the secret passage," she said.

The dowager focused on her again. "Excited? I should say so! After our brothers crowing over us, so sure they would find it before we did. And then, of course, they gave up after a couple of days. But we never gave up, did we, Margaret? Because we had the Secret Passage Society, and we'd taken our vow."

"And where did the passage lead, my lady?" asked Nancy.

But the dowager just gave her a wild stare. "Where are our notebooks, Margaret?" She gripped the arms of her chair and looked wildly around the room. "Where are our SPS notebooks? Did we leave them in the strong room?"

"So the passage leads to the strong room?"

The dowager stood up in distress. "Our notebooks!"

"I'll find them, don't worry," said Nancy, taking the old lady's arm in a firm grip. "Let's go into the drawing room and look at your shells, my lady. Tell me about your visit to Osborne House again."

The dowager allowed Nancy to lead her into

the drawing room and settle her on a sofa. Nancy fetched the box of shells and laid it gently on her lap. As she lifted the lid, the old lady gave her an intense conspiratorial look.

"We'll never tell a soul, will we, Margaret?" she said, putting her finger to her lips. "What a wonderful secret we have."

When Nancy walked into the servants' hall for lunch, Rosa's chair was empty. Her stomach clenched in dread.

"Where's Rosa?" she asked.

Mr Armitage was carving a chicken. He paused for a second before saying, "Rosa has left."

Florence jerked her head up and stared at him. "Left? Why?"

"Don't ask questions, Florence," said Mrs Dawes.

"But how's Nancy going to manage on her own? With this big dinner coming up too."

"Mrs Dawes will engage a girl from the village," said the butler.

Nancy tried not to let her face betray anything, but she was flooded with anger and fear. The earl was wasting no time in getting his estate ready for Hitler. Thank goodness she had given Rosa that letter. She desperately hoped Rosa would do as she had asked and take it to her parents.

*If Rosa hands you this*, Nancy had written, *you will know she has been sacked from Stanbrook because she's Jewish – no other reason. Rosa doesn't know what's in this letter, but I overheard something that made me worry, so I asked her to bring it to you if anything happened. You know from all my letters that she's a lovely person, and I know you'll look after her until she gets another job. She'll be sure to work for her keep, so she won't be a burden. Thank you so much. I'll write properly soon. Your loving Nancy.*

How on earth was she going to stop Lord Evesham travelling to Ireland next week? Especially now that Sidney had deserted her. Should she try telling the police what she knew? She imagined their reaction if she told them she'd overheard the conversation while hiding under a dust sheet pretending to be a ghost.

No, there was only one way she could prove what Lord Evesham was planning. She had to find those pamphlets. She had already searched half the house. Now she would search the rest.

# CHAPTER TWENTY-FOUR

## Shattered

Sidney felt as though she was trapped in a nightmare from which she would never wake up. Her world was shattered, and her parents were each locked in their own private hell. She couldn't understand why she had been called home, since they barely seemed to notice she was there.

Her mother had retreated to her bedroom, refusing food, drink and consolation. Her father was trying to stay calm, but his eyes were glazed over, and often he didn't hear when Sidney spoke to him. He rarely spoke, and when he did, his voice was so quiet that she had to strain to hear his words. Once she walked into the kitchen to find him sitting at the table, silent tears running down his cheeks as he rubbed polish into his shoes. With a painful lump in her throat, she crept away, holding in her sobs until she reached her bedroom. She was used to him being distant and uncommunicative – her mother always said he had never been the same since he'd come back from the last war. She knew he suffered from nightmares and had to take medicine to help him sleep. But she had never seen him cry before.

Well-meaning neighbours visited with food, which was gratefully received, and words of advice, which were harder to swallow. Everybody told her that she needed to be strong for her mother; that her brother had died for his country and that by bearing up bravely and carrying on she would be honouring his memory.

It was impossible to believe she would never see George again; never hear his voice; never see his handwriting on a letter; never hear his laugh. Impossible to believe he was dead. Several times a day she would think of something she must tell him in her next letter, and then she would realise, and the realisation felt like falling into a bottomless pit. Who could she talk to now?

The nights were the worst. She lay awake for hours, tortured with horrible images. It was unbearable not to know where he was. Never to know where he was. Not to be able to bring him home, to lay him to rest in the village where he had grown up.

Had he even been buried? Or was he lying in a field somewhere, trampled by soldiers' boots?

She clamped her hands over her ears and burrowed under the bedclothes. *Stop it, Sidney. Stop picturing it.*

What was the point of anything if this was how it ended? What had been the point of George's life – his energy and humour, his cleverness and warmth – if it all ended with him abandoned, cold and alone, in an unknown field?

* * *

After almost a week at home, her father drove her back to the station. Neither of them said a word in the car. Sidney felt numb. She hoped the numbness would last. It was the only way she would be able to cope with school.

Her father set her bag down on the platform. "Your headmistress wants you to report to her when you arrive," he said. He gave her an absent-minded pat on the shoulder, said goodbye and walked slowly back to the car, his shoulders drooping. He looked decades older than when he had seen her off the last time.

Everyone was in lessons when she arrived, thank goodness. She was dreading the looks, the whispers, the nudges.

She knocked on Miss Hathersage's study door.

"Ah, Sidney, welcome back," said the headmistress. "I hope your time at home has not been too much of a strain. I'm sure it was a great comfort to your parents to have you there."

"Yes, madam," said Sidney.

"The way in which you conduct yourself will set an example to others. Your fellow pupils will look to you to be a model of dignity and restraint. We are all being asked to make sacrifices at the moment, and to put the common good above our individual happiness. See that you honour your brother's memory in your conduct, so that he would be proud of you."

"Yes, madam."

"Now go to your lesson. The routine of school will be an enormous help to you, I am sure."

Sidney's form was in the middle of a French lesson. She was grateful for the rule that girls who were late must not knock at the door or interrupt the lesson by explaining the reason for their lateness. The rule was to enter quietly and take one's seat, and then see the teacher at the end.

There was no sound from inside the classroom. Sidney opened the door as softly as she could. Several girls glanced up, but when they saw her they turned back to their work. Ginny nudged Phyllis and whispered something, but the teacher glared at them and they bent their heads back to their books. Mademoiselle Lardet gave Sidney a brief nod as she walked to her seat. The teacher looked older and more haggard than she had a week ago. The news from France was very bad. The French government had surrendered to Germany, leaving Britain as the only country in the world still fighting Hitler. Sidney wondered where Mademoiselle Lardet's family was and whether she had heard from them at all.

The girls were translating a passage of French into English. Mary, who sat next to Sidney, slid her textbook across to show her the page number. Sidney retrieved her things from her desk and flicked to the right page. She looked at the passage, but it was like looking at a language she had never seen before. She had no idea what it was or what on earth she was supposed to do with it.

There were no bells between lessons at Stanbrook,

so the girls had to rely on the teacher to notice the time. At three o'clock, Mademoiselle Lardet was still sitting completely motionless, her elbows on her desk and her head propped in her hands. As the corridor began to fill with the sounds of other classes coming out for break, several girls looked at their watches, then glanced at the teacher and each other. Mademoiselle Lardet didn't move. Lucinda cleared her throat pointedly. There was no reaction.

"Excuse me, mademoiselle," said Lucinda. "I think it's breaktime."

The teacher lifted her head from her hands as though it was exceptionally heavy. Her eyes were glassy and unfocused. She nodded. "You may go, girls."

They put their books away and filed out in silence. Once they were in the corridor, Lucinda said, "Honestly, I think she's lost her mind."

"She's probably worried sick about her family," said Mary. "It must be awful."

"Well, she's paid to teach us," said Lucinda, "and she's not even attempting to at the moment. I shall write to my mother about it."

As they walked out to the walled garden where they had their breaks, Ginny and Phyllis smiled awkwardly at Sidney and said hello. Lucinda ignored her completely. Other girls shot her covert glances and then either turned away or gave a quick embarrassed smile if she caught their eyes.

Who cared? What did it matter?

In the garden, standing at the edge of a group, she

was vaguely aware of the conversation.

"I say, Mary, do you remember that sweet Italian restaurant we dined at when you stayed with me last summer?" said Daphne.

"Oh yes, with the dreamy waiter," said Mary eagerly. "What was his name – Alberto or something?"

"Armando," said Daphne.

"Mm, Armando. Honestly, he looked like a film star. I nearly died when he smiled at me."

"Well, my mother wrote that when Italy declared war, their restaurant was smashed up by a terrible mob, and all the men were arrested and interned – the father and four sons. The mother is absolutely distraught, and she's had to close down the restaurant."

"Oh, that's so sad."

"It's ridiculous," said Daphne. "They've been living here for simply ages. As if they'd be on Hitler's side."

"I suppose the government has to intern all enemy aliens, though," said Patricia. "Just to be on the safe side. I mean, some of the Italians living here must be fascists, and they could be spying for Hitler."

A rush of white-hot rage surged through Sidney's body. Since the news of George's death, she had been so flooded with grief that there had been room for nothing else. But back here, with the girls discussing the war, it hit her like a blow to the stomach. Lord Evesham was going to Ireland on Friday to hand over the plans of every British airfield and aircraft factory to the Germans. And all George's friends would be in terrible danger.

"The people they should be arresting," Sidney said, "are the fifth columnists." Her hands trembled and her voice shook with anger. "The British people working to overturn the government and welcome the Nazis."

"But the government is rounding them up too," said Mary.

"Not enough of them. Some of them are still completely free."

Mary gave her a puzzled frown. "Like who?"

"Like—" Sidney stopped, suddenly aware that everyone was staring at her. She shook her head irritably. "It doesn't matter."

If they stared at her for one second longer, she would scream. She turned and strode out of the garden, powered by fury. For the first time in her life everything was absolutely clear to her. George had lost his life in the fight against fascism. The least she could do was fight for the truth.

# CHAPTER TWENTY-FIVE

# An Amazing Idea

Nancy stared at Sidney in horror.

"I'm so sorry. That's terrible."

Sidney nodded and swallowed. Her throat felt constricted.

"So you'd just had the news when I saw you outside the house that day?" Nancy asked. "You were going home?"

Sidney nodded.

"And I was so horrible," said Nancy, squirming at the memory of her furious outburst. "Why didn't you tell me?"

"I don't want to talk about it. I just want to destroy Lord Evesham."

"Shh!" Nancy glanced around in consternation.

Sidney had found her as Nancy was returning to the house at the end of her afternoon break. There didn't seem to be anyone close by, but you could never tell. Nancy led her to the middle of the South Lawn, where they couldn't be overheard if they kept their voices low.

"Are you sure you want to be involved?" Nancy

asked. "It's dangerous. He's not a nice man, to put it mildly."

"I don't care!"

"Shh, keep your voice down."

Sidney took a deep breath. "We have to stop him. If we don't, it's an insult to – to everyone who's stood up against the Nazis."

"I've been searching the house," said Nancy, "looking for those pamphlets he talked about."

Sidney gasped, her eyes huge. "Of course! That's the evidence we need! Did you find them?"

"No," said Nancy. "I've looked in all the rooms I could get into, and I've scoured the attics. I sneaked into the cellars too, but there was nothing. Though I couldn't get into the—"

"I know!" Sidney exclaimed, grabbing Nancy's arm.

"Sshh!" Nancy glanced around in panic, but there was no sign of anyone.

"Nancy, I know where the printing press is!"

Nancy frowned. "What? How?"

Sidney told Nancy what she had heard Lord Evesham and Dorothy Taylor discussing, and what she had seen from her dormitory window.

"I bet you anything it's in the stable," she said, her eyes wide and her face flushed with excitement. "So we need to break in and take some pamphlets."

Nancy stared at her. Sidney seemed to be a completely different person. Did bereavement do that to you? And did it last, or was it just the shock? Would she go back to being like she was before? And if so, would she desert Nancy and betray her?

"What if there aren't any pamphlets in the stable, though?" Nancy said. "Like you said, he might be hiding them in the house."

"But you've already spent ages searching. I bet you anything they're in the stable. Can you get hold of tools to help us break in? We'll need to go in the dead of night. I tried snooping around before in daylight and he caught me."

"What?" said Nancy, horrified.

"Yes, it wasn't very nice. He was pretty frightening actually. Said something threatening about not being able to guarantee my safety if he caught me trespassing again."

"But night-time's when he does his printing. He said so."

"I'm sure he doesn't do it every night. We'll just have to hope he's not there tonight."

"We can't rush into this. It's not a schoolgirl prank."

Sidney glowered. "I'm well aware of that, thank you."

"We need to think it through. What are we going to do with the pamphlets once we have them? If we're taking such a risk to get them, we need to have a proper plan."

"We'll take them to the police station, of course," Sidney said.

"Don't give me that condescending tone. Remember what the police were like when I telephoned them? And what if they think we're mixed up in something ourselves? There was an article in the paper this morning about a man being put in prison for three months for trying to give an airman a Nazi pamphlet."

"But it's not only the pamphlets. We can ask them to come and see the printing press in Lord Evesham's stable."

"I'm still not sure they'd take us seriously. Do you really think they'll come and arrest Lord Evesham? Upper-class men like him can get away with anything. I've seen it all my life. I don't think the local police would have the guts to take him on. Can you imagine Lord Evesham allowing the Stanbrook constable to investigate his stables? Can you imagine the local police actually arresting the Earl of Stanbrook? I can't."

Sidney's optimism deflated like a leaky balloon. "But surely they'd pass the leaflets on to the chief constable to investigate? Or Scotland Yard..." She faltered.

"Maybe. Or maybe they'd say they would, and then the leaflets would quietly disappear and he'd be allowed to carry on exactly as before."

Sidney drew in her breath. "Do you remember what he said about the chief constable, though? When he was talking to that woman in the Long Gallery? What was her name?"

"Dorothy Taylor," said Nancy, with that sick feeling that the thought of Dorothy Taylor always gave her these days.

"He said most of the police support him," said

Sidney, "but there's a bad patch up above, including the local chief constable, who's a staunch supporter of Churchill. I remember his exact words, because I was thinking how topsy-turvy he was. When he said a bad patch, he meant people who don't support fascism. So—"

Nancy gasped. An extraordinary picture was forming in her head.

"What?" Sidney asked.

"Do you remember him saying about this dinner he's giving for all the county bigwigs on Thursday? Lord-lieutenant, high sheriff, chief constable, MPs, all that lot?"

"Yes. So what?"

"Don't you see? Those are *exactly* the people we need to tell. He's planning to destroy the whole government, which is full of people of his own class. They won't let him get away with that. The last thing the people in power want is a revolution that would take away their power. So if we can show his dinner guests what he's planning, surely they'd turn against him? I bet they'd all be horrified. That's why he's so against the dinner. He said the chief constable supports Churchill. I bet the others do too."

"But what's your plan?" said Sidney. "We can't just storm into his dinner party. We'd be thrown out instantly, then I'd be expelled and you'd be sacked. Nice plan, Nancy."

Nancy itched to smack her. "Don't patronise me," she said. "We wouldn't storm in. I just had an amazing idea. You know how they were talking about dropping their fascist pamphlets over cities from aeroplanes?"

Sidney frowned. "Yes?"

"So we can do the same! Not from aeroplanes obviously, but there's that balcony all round the library, and there's a door on to the balcony from the first-floor landing. We can creep in there and then drop the leaflets from the balcony while they're having their dinner, and tell all the guests what we've seen and heard."

Sidney stared at her, eyes wide. "That might actually work."

"So we have to find that printing press and take some pamphlets," said Nancy. "Hundreds of pamphlets, enough to shower all over the dinner table, so they can't possibly ignore them."

## CHAPTER TWENTY-SIX

# A Torch and a Pistol

Clocks struck midnight all over the house as Sidney tiptoed down the back staircase to the servants' basement. Below ground-floor level there were no lights, and she had to feel her way with her feet. Finally she inched a foot forward and, instead of finding the edge of a stair, it slid along solid ground.

Where was Nancy? She had definitely said to meet at the bottom of the stairs, hadn't she? What if she'd slept through her alarm?

*Please come*, Sidney prayed. She really didn't want to go through all this again tomorrow. Besides, tomorrow was Wednesday, and the dinner was on Thursday. They had no time to lose.

Was that a light? Yes, a flickering light was casting spooky shadows on the wall further up the stairwell. At the turn in the staircase, a foot appeared on a stair, followed by the rest of Nancy, holding a candle in an enamel saucer. Sidney's heart thumped and her stomach lurched at the thought of what they were about to do.

Nancy's face was grim and tense. She motioned

impatiently to Sidney. Sidney frowned, and then realised she was standing right in front of the door. She moved aside to let Nancy slowly lift the heavy latch. She held her breath in case the door creaked, but it opened silently.

They stepped out into a stone-flagged passage. Sidney closed the door and followed Nancy to the end of the corridor. Nancy slid back three heavy bolts on the outside door, and they crept out and up the steps into the moonlit night. Sidney shivered and buttoned up the cardigan she was wearing over her nightdress.

Nancy blew out her candle and left the saucer on the steps. She led the way to the stable yard. A bat fluttered in front of Sidney's face and she just about stopped herself from shrieking.

No light came from the stables, but as they drew closer Sidney heard muffled clunking, rattling and squeaking sounds. The girls stared at each other. Sidney's heart was racing. He was in there right now, churning out his fascist pamphlets. There was no way they'd be able to get the pamphlets tonight.

Sidney felt a sneeze prickling at her nose. *Oh no, not now, please!* She turned away and pressed her hands over her face, clamping her mouth shut, but the sneeze was forcing its way out.

"AAAAAAAAATISHOOO!"

They froze for a second. Then Nancy grabbed her arm. "Run!" she whispered.

Racing away, Sidney glanced back in panic as the stable door flew open and light spilled into the yard.

Lord Evesham appeared in the doorway, a torch in one hand and a pistol in the other.

Before the torch beam caught them they sprinted into the little wood between the stable yard and the gardens. Sidney turned cold with horror as she heard Lord Evesham's footsteps pounding behind them.

"Quick," urged Nancy, veering down a narrow, overgrown path. Sidney tore after her, but her cardigan caught on a patch of brambles. She tugged but it wouldn't come free, and looking back she saw Lord Evesham's torch beam zigzagging around the wood. She frantically undid the buttons and raced on to catch up with Nancy, leaving the cardigan stuck in the brambles.

At the far side of the wood, they clambered over a low wall and found themselves at the edge of the lawn. Nancy led Sidney to a huge yew hedge.

"In here," she whispered.

They wriggled their way into the hedge to a little gap in the centre where the old yew had died back. They huddled on the ground as Lord Evesham's torch beam shone across the lawn.

His footsteps brushed the grass close by. They bent their heads so their faces were covered by their hair. Thank goodness her nightdress was navy blue, Sidney thought. And with Nancy's dark green dress, they should be pretty well camouflaged.

Lord Evesham shone his torch into the dense yew. Sidney held her breath. But the torch beam wasn't powerful enough to reach the middle of the hedge. With a relief that made her light-headed,

Sidney saw the beam swing back on to the lawn as the footsteps continued.

*Thank you, thank you!* she silently repeated. *Thank yew*, she thought, and smiled to herself at the pun. She must write that to George.

Her stomach clenched as she remembered. No. Mustn't think about that.

Where was Lord Evesham?

The gardens were silent apart from the hooting of owls. Neither of them stirred. Sidney had pins and needles in her legs, but she didn't dare move.

After some time, they saw the torch beam coming back in their direction. It zigzagged across the lawn and gave a cursory sweep along the hedge, before disappearing round the corner.

Had he given up?

Still neither of them moved. Sidney's pins and needles were excruciating now. Something rustled in the hedge nearby. She hoped it was a hedgehog, not a rat.

Nancy raised her head. "I think he's gone," she whispered.

Sidney shifted her weight and rubbed her painful legs to get them working again. The thought of venturing out into the open and being caught by Lord Evesham, armed with a pistol, gave her a hollow feeling inside.

But they couldn't stay here all night. She had no idea what time it was, but the sun rose ridiculously early at the moment. They needed to go back while it was still dark.

"Ready?" asked Nancy.

Sidney nodded.

The journey back was terrifying, but there was no sign of Lord Evesham. Sidney crept to the dormitory and climbed into bed, shaking with relief. They had got away with it.

She woke just before the rising bell on Wednesday morning, and a hideous vision came into her head.

Her cardigan, spreadeagled inside out on the brambles. And, sewn on in her mother's neat stitches, the name tape with its blue woven letters: SIDNEY DASHWORTH.

Oh no, oh no, oh no!

Heart racing, she scrambled out of bed and pulled on her uniform with shaking hands.

"What are you in such a hurry for?" said Ginny, yawning.

Phyllis sat up, blinked at Sidney and frowned. "Why do you have a twig in your hair?"

"I don't," said Sidney as she shoved her feet into her shoes and left. In the corridor she hastily tied her laces and hurried downstairs, running her fingers through her hair to find the twig.

It was a perfect summer morning, blue skies and birds singing, as she raced over to the copse and up the path. She walked the entire way along it and back again before, dizzy with dread, she finally admitted the truth to herself.

Her cardigan had gone.

# Daily Herald

# 1,250,000 TROOPS TO RESIST INVASION

Britain's "inflexible resolve" to continue the war was expressed by Mr Winston Churchill in the House of Commons last night in the most fateful and dramatic speech that he has ever made.

"The Battle of France is over," he said. "The Battle of Britain is about to begin...

"The whole fury and might of the enemy must very soon be turned upon us.

"Hitler knows he will have to break us in this island or lose the war.

"If we can stand up to him, all Europe may be free and the life of the world may move forward into broad, sunlit uplands.

"But if we fail, then the whole world, including the United States, including all that we have known and cared for, will sink into the abyss of a new Dark Age...

"Let us therefore brace ourselves to our duties, and so bear ourselves that if the British Commonwealth lasts for a thousand years, men will still say, 'This was their finest hour.'"

# CHAPTER TWENTY-SEVEN

## Never Again

At the end of Breakfast Notices, Miss Rutter said, "And finally, girls, I have an exciting announcement to make. Lord Evesham is holding an important dinner tomorrow night, a long-accustomed tradition in which the new Earl of Stanbrook plays host to all the local dignitaries. I am delighted to announce that his lordship has done us the enormous honour of requesting that the school form a welcoming party for the guests."

There was a buzz of excitement around the room. Miss Rutter held up her hand for silence and proceeded to give a long list of instructions about the expected standards of appearance and behaviour. Sidney didn't listen. Dread had settled like a stone in her chest, making it difficult to breathe normally, let alone pay attention to anything.

After breakfast, they went to clean their teeth and change for their drilling class. Sidney was alone in the dormitory, lacing up her gym shoes, when Ginny and Phyllis burst in, toothbrushes and toothpaste in their hands. Phyllis's cheeks were blotchy and

Ginny's face was tight with fury.

"That's it," said Ginny. "I'm never speaking to her again."

"Who?" asked Sidney.

"Lucinda, of course. She's been absolutely beastly to Phyllis."

"What did she do?"

Phyllis burst into tears. "She said I've got fat knees and no eyebrows."

"What an absolute cow," said Sidney.

Lucinda had ignored her since her return to school. No eye contact, nothing. It was as if she had decided Sidney didn't exist. It was a blessed relief and, with any luck, would be a permanent state of affairs.

"We're not going to let her get away with it any longer," said Ginny. "We'll send her to Coventry. Are you in, Sidney?"

"With pleasure."

Lucinda walked into the room. Ginny and Phyllis turned their backs on her and started getting changed.

"Sending me to Coventry, are you?" scoffed Lucinda. "Such babies. Honestly, Phyllis, if you can't take a few home truths, you need to grow up. I only said it for your own good."

"Huh!" said Sidney.

Lucinda rounded on her, her face distorted with loathing. "Shut up, you frizzy-haired freak."

"Don't call her that," said Phyllis.

Sidney stared at Phyllis in astonishment.

"*Don't call her that,*" Lucinda parroted in a

weedy high-pitched voice that was clearly meant to be an imitation of Phyllis's. "Trying to stand up for her, are you? How sweet. You're pathetic, Phyllis Lethbridge, do you know that?"

A look came over Phyllis that Sidney had never seen before. She turned white and her face hardened. She stood up and fixed Lucinda with an expression of cold fury.

"No, you're the one who's pathetic. Trying to make yourself feel good by making other people feel bad. Laughing and sneering and mocking. The only reason anyone puts up with you is because you're so nasty that they're scared to get on the wrong side of you. You've insulted me and jeered at me ever since I started at St Olave's, and I've tried to ignore it and never answered back, because I was frightened that if I said anything you'd be even nastier. And you're right. That was pathetic. But you know what? You're a loathsome human being, Lucinda Gore-Withers, and I will never, ever put up with your bullying again."

Sidney watched, spellbound, as Lucinda actually backed away from the torrent of Phyllis's scorn. By the time Phyllis had finished, she had almost reached the doorway. Speechless, Lucinda left the room.

Phyllis sank down on her bed. Her hands were shaking.

"Well done, Phyllis!" said Sidney. "That was incredible."

"I feel sick," said Phyllis. "My heart's beating

so fast."

"That was so brave," said Ginny. "You were amazing."

Phyllis looked dazed. "I don't know what happened. It was like I was possessed. Who was it in the story where the scales fell from their eyes and instantly they could see clearly? I just saw her sneering face and the scales fell from my eyes, and suddenly I couldn't understand how I'd put up with her nastiness all this time."

"It was amazing," said Ginny again. "The look on her face!"

"It's going to be awful now, isn't it?" said Phyllis. "I bet she'll report me to Miss Hathersage, and then I'll be expelled."

"She won't report you," said Sidney.

"Why do you say that?"

"Because everything you said is true, and she knows it. Look at how she backed out of the room like a wounded animal. I'm sure she won't report you."

"Do you think so? I hope you're right. Gosh, the atmosphere's going to be hideous, though, isn't it? Sorry."

Sidney shrugged. What did it matter?

As she made her way to drilling class, a hopeful thought suddenly struck her. What if Lord Evesham *hadn't* found her cardigan? What if a gardener had found it instead, and had returned it to the school as lost property? Surely if Lord Evesham had found it, he would have reported her to Miss

Hathersage, and she would have been summoned by now. It looked very much as though she had got away with it.

But the dinner was tomorrow night. How on earth would they get hold of those pamphlets now?

# CHAPTER TWENTY-EIGHT

# You'll Regret This

Sidney took her place between Ginny and Phyllis, waiting for drilling class to begin.

Perhaps the gardener's boy who'd told her about the secret passage had found her cardigan. She remembered how excited she'd been at the thought of discovering a secret passage. How long ago it seemed. And yet only a few weeks had passed since then.

The image that haunted her, of George lying abandoned in a muddy field, flashed into her head. She tried to force it out.

"I've been thinking, Sidney," whispered Ginny. "That night when you dared us to come to the Long Gallery."

"Hmm?" Sidney stood perfectly still, her eyes looking straight ahead, as Miss Newsom surveyed the students like a sergeant major inspecting his troops.

"It seems rather a coincidence that you dared us to go down there on the very night the statue came alive. Especially when it only happens once a year.

Don't you think that's extraordinary?"

"Mm."

What seemed extraordinary to Sidney was that Ginny was still going on about something that had happened in another life. She had absolutely no interest in the statue prank any more.

"Attention, girls!" called Miss Newsom. "Stand on the spot and stretch both arms straight above your heads. Take deep breaths of this beautiful, healthful air."

Ginny turned to Phyllis. "Look," she whispered, arms stretched high. "Lord Evesham with the Sage."

Sidney's legs trembled. Sure enough, Lord Evesham was walking on to the lawn with the headmistress.

This was it then.

"Lift your right leg off the ground and balance on your left leg," called Miss Newsom. "Straight backs, firm posture."

Lord Evesham and Miss Hathersage made their way towards the teacher.

"Move your arms out to the sides, level with your shoulders," Miss Newsom instructed.

Sidney wobbled and lowered her right foot to steady herself.

"Firm posture, Sidney!" called Miss Newsom.

Lord Evesham glanced at the teacher and turned sharply to see who she was talking to. Sidney was shaking far too much to lift her foot again. Lord Evesham pointed at her and said something to Miss Hathersage, who nodded. Sidney gave up any attempt to balance on one leg. She stood with her head bent and her teeth chattering.

With one final glance at Sidney, Lord Evesham left the lawn. Miss Hathersage said something to Miss Newsom and then walked back towards the house. Miss Newsom stepped forward to face the ranks of girls.

"Sidney Dashworth, please report to the headmistress's study immediately."

"I understand, of course, that you are in a state of shock, and shock can lead people to behave in highly inappropriate ways," said Miss Hathersage in a patronising tone that made Sidney want to hit her. "But really, Sidney, to leave your bed and wander about the grounds in your nightdress!" She gave an exaggerated shudder. "Such appallingly undignified behaviour. And then, when Lord Evesham saw you during his nightly check of the blackout, to run away through the woods! You can only imagine my mortification when his lordship reported your behaviour to me. It is hardly the conduct I expect from one of my pupils."

"Yes, madam."

So that was what Lord Evesham had told her, was it? Nightly check of the blackout indeed.

"I did explain your recent circumstances to his lordship," the headmistress continued, "and he was most graciously sympathetic. But he insisted – quite rightly, of course – that you must be removed from the school. He thoughtfully suggested that perhaps an institution might be the best place for you at the moment, since the strain of looking after a daughter who is not in her right mind, especially one who cannot be trusted to remain in bed at night, might be too much for your parents."

*What?!* Lord Evesham was trying to have her sent to an *asylum*?!

Consumed with fury, Sidney banged her hands on Miss Hathersage's desk.

"Lord Evesham is a fascist!" she burst out. "He's going to overthrow the government and set up a Nazi dictatorship in Britain as soon as the Germans invade. I heard him!"

Two red spots appeared in the headmistress's cheeks. Sidney spoke quickly, desperate to tell her story before she was stopped.

"He's used his job at the Air Ministry to get hold of the plans for every airfield and aircraft factory in Britain and he's flying to Ireland on Friday to hand them to the Germans. He's got a printing press in the stables, and he's printing pamphlets to announce his new regime. He's going to drop them all over the country from aeroplanes. That's what we – I mean, I – was looking for last night. *That's* why he wants me locked up. He caught me trying to get into the stable before, and he knows I know what he's up to."

Miss Hathersage rose from her seat, her face rigid with anger.

"You have to listen to me," Sidney begged. "You have to believe me. I can show you the stable. You can ask the police to break in and find the printing press. You can do what you like to me, but you have to report him to the police."

Miss Hathersage was trembling with rage. "I see now that you are very sick indeed. Go to your dormitory and pack your overnight bag, then go directly to the station. Your trunk will be sent on later. I shall telephone your parents and let them know that you are travelling home today and will not be returning to the school. I shall recommend that they make arrangements for you to spend some time in an institution."

"There's no need to telephone my parents," Sidney said. "I can explain to them myself."

She turned to leave, but as she opened the door the fury overcame her and she whipped round to face the headmistress.

"You'll regret this, Miss Hathersage. When Hitler invades, and we're overrun by the Nazis like the rest of Europe, and people are being executed and sent to prison camps, you'll regret that you were the person who let it happen, all because you didn't have the decency to believe one of your own pupils. Goodbye."

And she closed the door behind her and strode down the corridor.

# CHAPTER TWENTY-NINE

## There Might
## Be a Way

What could she do now? She couldn't possibly go back home. What if her parents believed Miss Hathersage and had her locked up? She had heard of girls her age being put in institutions. And maybe her parents would be relieved to get rid of her. They clearly had no interest in her at the moment.

She *had* to find those pamphlets and expose Lord Evesham. But she couldn't do that if she wasn't here.

As she trudged up to her dormitory, Nancy came down the stairs, carrying her cleaning box. She glanced up and down the stairs warily, and then, in a low voice, she said, "I was hoping to see you. I saw his lordship in the basement this morning. Walking along the corridor from the cellars."

Sidney frowned. "So?"

"He never goes down to the cellars. He gets Mr Armitage to do all his donkey work. So he must have been doing something he doesn't want Mr A to know about. I think he's locked the pamphlets in the strong room."

"What?"

"He knows somebody's on to him, doesn't he? He knows someone was snooping around the stable block last night. He didn't see us, so he doesn't know it was just a couple of schoolgirls. He probably thinks it was Secret Service agents or spies. So he won't risk keeping his pamphlets in the stables any more, will he? I bet he's taken them to the strong room. He's got dozens of boxes full of priceless vases and stuff in there. I saw the removal men bring them into the house. He could easily hide a few boxes of pamphlets in with those."

"But what about the printing press? He can't have carried that to the strong room on his own."

"I bet he'll move it away from Stanbrook. He might have moved it already. So there's no time to lose. We need to get to the strong room and find the pamphlets. And I might know a way we can do that. Guess what, there might be a secret passage! The dowager was—"

Sidney put up her hand to stop her. She couldn't cope with any more words.

"I've been expelled," she said.

Nancy's eyebrows shot up. "What?"

"I left my cardigan in the bushes and it had a name tape in it. Lord Evesham found it and I've been expelled. I'm just going to get my stuff."

Nancy's face was white. "You idiot! You just don't *think*, do you? First you gave us away by sneezing—"

"How is that my fault? I couldn't help sneezing!"

"And then you go and leave your cardigan on a

bush for him to find!"

"It got tangled in the brambles when we were running through the woods. If I hadn't left it, he'd have caught me."

"He caught you anyway! Did you tell them I was there too?"

"Of course I didn't! I'm not a sneak. Miss Hathersage just thinks I've gone mad with grief or something and I'm wandering around in my nightgown like the Lady in Grey. She wants my parents to put me in an asylum. So you can shut up, thank you. I've got quite enough to worry about without your nasty accusations."

Sidney turned and ran back down the stairs. Her head felt as though it was exploding. She had no idea what to do, but she had to get out of here.

She strode down the drive, oblivious to the world around her, locked inside her whirling mind. How could she possibly stop Lord Evesham now?

"Excuse me, miss."

Sidney looked up to see a girl of about her own age in a cotton dress and sandals, carrying a small cardboard suitcase.

"Excuse me, but are you from Stanbrook House?" She spoke in a local accent like Nancy's.

"Kind of," said Sidney.

"I don't suppose you know which door I should use? I'm starting work here, and I had no idea it would be so big." She gestured towards the enormous building. "I have to ask for Mrs Dawes, but I don't know which entrance I'm meant to go to."

"Are you the new housemaid?" Sidney asked. Nancy had told her that Rosa had been sacked.

"Yes," said the girl. "Only temporary, like. My mum heard they needed a maid urgently. I've already got a job starting Monday, but Mum said I could do this in the meantime. She didn't want me hanging around the house, and she needs the money."

Sidney's mind was racing. "You don't sound very keen on the job."

"I'm not. My aunt invited me to stay with her in Oxford before I started work, but Mum made me take this job instead. I've never been to Oxford and now I never will."

Sidney looked at her thoughtfully. "I'm not so sure," she said. "There might be a way you could go to Oxford after all."

"Oh, there you are, Nancy," said Florence, opening the door of the library, where Nancy was kneeling under the table with a dustpan and brush. "The temporary maid's here. I've sorted her out with her uniform and box. Keep her with you today, will you, and show her the ropes?"

She turned to the new girl. "Right, Elsie, Nancy will look after you. I'll see you at lunchtime."

Nancy straightened up and got her first look at the new girl.

"This is Elsie," said Florence. "What's up, Nancy? You look as though you've seen a ghost."

# CHAPTER THIRTY

# Right Under His Nose

Nancy looked utterly bewildered. She seemed to have lost the power of speech.

"I couldn't leave you here by yourself to deal with Lord Evesham," said Sidney, still tingling with excitement at her extraordinary change of direction. "And I couldn't go home. And then I met the new maid coming up the drive, and I had this amazing idea. We had to swap clothes in the woods – her aunt will be so confused when she turns up in St Olave's uniform. And she doesn't know anybody here – I checked with her – so nobody will know I'm not her."

"Until one of the schoolgirls recognises you."

"I'll make sure they don't. I know the times they use the stairs, and I'll stay away."

"And what if his lordship sees you?"

Sidney's legs felt wobbly at the thought, but she tried to sound unconcerned. "You said yourself, servants are invisible to the family. And you don't clean his rooms while he's in them, surely? I thought you'd be pleased. I came back to help you expose him."

"It's a massive risk. You being here, right under his nose."

"But it's only until tomorrow night. We just have to get hold of those pamphlets and drop them from the balcony, and make sure the right people have proof of what he's up to."

"You make it sound easy."

"That's not what I meant."

"You'll have to change your accent. Otherwise you'll be found out the moment you open your mouth."

"I already did, when I arrived. Florence didn't seem suspicious, did she, so it must have been all right. And I won't talk more than I need to. I can pretend to be shy."

"What are you going to do about your parents? If the headmistress has telephoned them, they'll be expecting you home today. Then they'll get worried and telephone the school, and there'll be no end of a fuss."

Sidney's stomach lurched. "I wasn't really thinking that far ahead."

Nancy appeared to be about to retort, but then she seemed to change her mind. "Could you telephone them and say you're going to stay with a relative for a few days? Your grandparents, or an aunt or somebody?"

"Not really. It would seem awfully strange. And they'd be bound to telephone to check the arrangements, and then they'd find out."

"What if you telephoned to say you'd been allowed to stay after all?"

Sidney screwed up her mouth in thought. "They'd expect to hear that from the headmistress, though."

"You could say the headmistress is writing to explain. That will give you a couple of days before they suspect anything."

Sidney nodded slowly. "That might just work. Yes, that's a good idea. When will I be able to telephone them?"

"If Mrs Dawes doesn't give us too much mending after lunch, we should get a bit of time off this afternoon. You could walk to the telephone box then."

"All right. I'll do that. Now, tell me what you were saying about the pamphlets. You think he's put them in the strong room?"

Nancy shrugged. "That's my hunch. It's a bit of a coincidence that he was down there this morning. He looked really mad when he saw me."

"What were you saying about a secret passage?"

Nancy shrugged. "It might be nothing. Just something the dowager said when I was cleaning her dressing room. But she's dotty, poor old thing. She's convinced I'm her friend from sixty years ago."

"What did she say?"

"She suddenly got up and tried to move this massive wardrobe away from the wall. She was really upset that someone had put it there – it's one of those old panelled walls – and then she said, 'How will we get in now?'"

Sidney gasped. "So the secret passage is behind her wardrobe?"

"Maybe. But she says all sorts of stuff."

"The gardener's boy – Albert – he told me there's a secret passage that leads to the strong room."

Nancy's eyes widened. "*Albert* told *you*? When?"

"When we were gardening. He said his grandad who used to work here told him. I was planning to look for it, but then everything else happened."

"So we need to look behind the wardrobe," said Nancy. "And the dinner's tomorrow, so we need to do it today."

"Is the dowager in the room while you're cleaning?"

"Sometimes she is. And Miss Morris is always around. She'd certainly notice if I started moving the wardrobe."

"So it would have to be tonight, when they're both asleep."

They stared at each other, as the enormity of their plans began to sink in.

"So the wardrobe is in the dowager's dressing room," said Sidney.

"Yes. And her bedroom's next to the dressing room obviously. I know she takes a sleeping draught at night, so perhaps she'd sleep through us moving the wardrobe. Miss Morris's bedroom is on the other side of the dowager's, so she wouldn't hear unless we made a racket."

"And can we get into the apartment at night? Is it locked?"

Nancy looked at Sidney in dismay. "Yes. Miss Morris locks it. I have to knock when I go up in the morning, and I hear her unlocking it."

"Is there any way you could get hold of a spare key?"

"I suppose I could look in the dowager's bureau when I take in the supper tray."

"Won't they be in the room then?"

"No, that's when Miss Morris is helping her get ready for bed. I just leave the tray in the drawing room."

"So you'd have a bit of time."

"Maybe, but not much. And if she caught me rifling through drawers, I'd be thrown out of the house instantly."

"And there's no guarantee you'd find a spare key anyway."

"No."

Sidney thought hard. "Is the key left in the lock?"

"Yes, it's always in the lock."

"So when you take the supper tray in, you could just take the key?"

Nancy gave her a withering look. "Oh yes, that's a great idea. So when Miss Morris comes in five minutes later to lock up, and the key's gone, she'll never suspect the servant who's just left the room. The servant who's the only other person that ever goes in there."

"All right, there's no need to be sarcastic. I was only thinking aloud."

"Well, if your thoughts are that stupid, you'd be

better off keeping them to yourself."

Sidney gave her a look. "You can be as nasty as Lucinda sometimes, did you know that?"

"You're a fine one to talk."

"Well, you think of something then. Because if we don't get our hands on those pamphlets, we've got no chance of proving what he's up to and making sure his plans are stopped."

"Wait!" said Nancy. "It's obvious!"

"What is?"

Nancy's eyes were shining with excitement. "After I've taken in the supper tray, I go straight on up to bed. I don't go back down to the kitchen."

Sidney frowned in puzzlement. "So?"

"So ... I walk into the dowager's drawing room and leave the tray on the table. But I don't have to walk back out again, do I?"

# CHAPTER THIRTY-ONE

## Behind the Wardrobe

As the clocks struck eleven, Nancy crept out from behind a Chinese screen. Luckily her eyes had had a while to adjust to the dark, and she could just make out the shapes of the furniture as she felt her way to the door.

She turned the key carefully. There was a quiet clunk as the lock slid back. Nancy opened the door, and there was Sidney, sitting cross-legged in the dark corridor. She gave Nancy a thumbs-up sign as she switched on her torch and got to her feet.

Nancy led her through the drawing room and past the silent bedrooms. She held her breath as she inched the dressing-room door open, terrified it would squeak. But it opened soundlessly. Sidney closed it behind her and shone the weak torch beam around the room. Nancy pointed to the big oak wardrobe against the right-hand wall. Sidney nodded.

Switching the light on would have made things much easier, but Nancy didn't dare. So Sidney held the torch between her teeth while they each gripped a corner of the exposed end of the wardrobe.

"One, two, three, *lift*," whispered Nancy.

The wardrobe didn't budge.

"Try harder," Nancy ordered. "You're not pulling your weight."

"I am! I'm trying my hardest."

"Rubbish. I didn't spend two hours hiding behind a screen, risking my job, just to be defeated by a lazy weakling of a schoolgirl."

"It's heavy!" hissed Sidney.

"Of course it is! Use your muscles. If you've got any."

Sidney shot her a furious look.

"Grip it really tight," said Nancy. "One, two, three, *lift*."

They lifted the wardrobe a fraction and moved it a few inches away from the panelling before Sidney had to let go.

"Good," whispered Nancy. "Again."

As they set it down this time, there was a rattling of coat hangers from inside the wardrobe. Bedsprings creaked in the room next door. They froze in terror.

"No," muttered the dowager. "No."

They waited, not daring to breathe, until the bedroom settled into silence.

"One more try," whispered Nancy. "Put your back into it."

They grasped the corners again and pulled it a few inches further out. Not far, but enough to squeeze behind it and investigate the panelling.

"Start at the top that end and work your way

down every panel until we meet in the middle," Nancy whispered.

They worked their way along the wall, pressing every corner of every panel. They all felt disappointingly solid. Then Nancy pressed the bottom right-hand corner of the centre panel and, to her amazement, the corner pushed inwards. They heard a small click, and a section made up of four panels sprang out a few inches from the rest, forming a little door halfway up the wall.

"Wow," breathed Sidney. "It does exist."

Nancy's heart was thumping. They had done it!

They stared at each other in the dim light, eyes huge, cheeks flushed. Neither of them could speak for a moment. Then Sidney whispered, "Shall we look inside?"

Nancy's stomach churned as she nodded. What if there was something terrible in there? But then she remembered that the last people who had been in there were Margaret and the dowager countess, and she stopped being frightened. She curled her fingers round the panels and pulled the door slowly open, praying it wouldn't creak.

It opened silently, revealing a black hole. Nancy felt cold air on her face, and a damp musty smell reached her nostrils. They stood side by side as Sidney shone her torch into the opening.

The beam lit up a curved brick wall a few feet behind the panelling. Sidney shone the torch upwards, showing a ceiling above them.

She shone the torch downwards.

They gasped.

Beneath them, twisting down and down and down, burrowing right through the middle of the house, was a steep, narrow spiral staircase.

# CHAPTER THIRTY-TWO

# Through the Panelling

"You go first," whispered Sidney. "You found it."

Nancy suspected that Sidney was saying this out of fear rather than generosity, but she was happy to obey. Whatever there was to see, she wanted to be the first to see it.

She stood on tiptoe and swung her right leg over the panelling. For the thousandth time, she wished she could wear trousers instead of a stupid dress. She felt for the first tread on the staircase and gingerly tested her weight. It seemed solid enough.

Instead of a banister rail, there was a thick rope threaded through rusty metal rings screwed into the wall. Nancy grasped it and swung her other leg over the panelling.

"Hand me the torch," she whispered. "Be careful. It looks all right, but some of the treads might be rotten."

She made her way down a few of the rough, splintered stairs, then turned and shone the torch on the steps above so Sidney could see her way.

In the weak light, Nancy glimpsed a narrow

ledge built into the wall. On the ledge lay two little cloth-bound notebooks. She shone the torch on the dusty red cover of the top one. In faded ink in beautiful Gothic script was written:

*Frederica Coverley*
*SPS*

Nancy gently lifted the notebook. The one beneath was identical, except on the cover was written:

*Margaret Pemberton*
*SPS*

A shiver ran down her spine. Some part of those two girls from sixty years ago lay right here at her fingertips.

"What is it?" asked Sidney, coming up behind her.

"Nothing," said Nancy, slipping the books into her apron pocket. "Just some old notebooks."

They climbed down and down the twisting staircase, until finally the torch beam revealed a brick floor at the bottom. Nancy shone the light around and the beam fell on a wooden door with a metal latch.

She turned hot and cold.

"Open it," urged Sidney.

But the latch wouldn't budge.

"It's stuck," Nancy said, frantically trying to wiggle it up and down and side to side.

"Let me try," said Sidney.

"If I can't move it, you'll never do it."

"Just let me try."

"Fine."

Nancy stepped aside, fizzing with pent-up frustration. Sidney pushed at the door with her shoulder while wiggling the latch to and fro. And finally the latch shot up and the door creaked ajar.

Nancy's stomach flipped. They had done it!

"It's so heavy," whispered Sidney, pushing on the door. "Feel it."

Nancy pushed. The door was incredibly heavy. It took all their strength to open it.

"Wow," breathed Sidney, as they stepped inside the room and shone the torch around.

On every side, piled high on shelves and pallets, sat boxes and packing cases of all shapes and sizes: Lord Evesham's priceless porcelain collection, and, perhaps, thousands of pamphlets that would incriminate him beyond all doubt.

Nancy turned to Sidney and saw why it had taken so much strength to open the door. Fixed to the inside of it was a sturdy old bookcase that stretched from floor to ceiling. Its shelves were stacked with boxes, and it completely hid the door behind it.

Sidney started to push the bookcase back.

"No!" yelled Nancy.

Sidney gave her a startled look that quickly changed to one of horror. She grabbed the edge of the door with both hands and doubled over, one hand still clutching the door, the other pressed to her heart.

"Oh, I can't believe I nearly did that," she gasped.

"You idiot! We could have been walled up forever!" Nancy took a box from a shelf and wedged it in the doorway.

"We could have banged on the door," said Sidney. "The one that goes out to the basement corridor, I mean."

"Oh yes, and then have been thrown into prison for breaking into Lord Evesham's strong room. Nice one, Sidney." Then Nancy was struck by a thought so terrible that she had to hold on to a shelf to stop her legs buckling. "You didn't shut the panelling upstairs, did you?"

"Of course not. I'm not that much of an idiot."

Nancy was so weak with relief that she could only nod.

Sidney shone her torch beam around the room. "How on earth are we going to find the pamphlets?"

"The boxes with his porcelain in are all labelled," said Nancy. "I saw the labels when they arrived."

"So the boxes of pamphlets either won't be labelled, or, if he's clever, they'll have false labels, to make it seem as though they're art like the others."

"I hope he hasn't been that clever," said Nancy. "We can't prise open every box and rummage through the shavings. We're bound to spill some, and we'll never be able to clear them up."

"And if he's storing the pamphlets here, then he must be bringing in more boxes all the time," said Sidney. "So we can't leave any sign that we've been here."

Nancy's heart stopped. "Imagine if he comes while we're here! We didn't think of that."

"We'll keep an ear out," said Sidney. "We'd hear him unlocking the door from the basement, and we could just run for the secret passage. He can't know it exists, or he wouldn't keep his treasures here."

"I know!" said Nancy. "We'll weigh them!"

"What?"

"We'll lift every box. Each piece of porcelain will be packed in shavings, and there'll only be a few pieces in each box, so they'll be quite light."

"But a box of pamphlets will be really heavy!" said Sidney. "Of course! Nancy, you're a genius!"

Nancy shrugged, trying to hide her pleasure. "Let's work our way round in opposite directions. It's going to take hours."

# CHAPTER THIRTY-THREE

# The Only Hope
# We've Got

It did take hours. The girls worked their way around the entire room, but they didn't lift a single box that felt heavy enough to be stuffed with pamphlets.

"He might have been really clever, of course," said Sidney, "and not have put too many in each box, and packed them in shavings, so they weigh the same as the porcelain."

"I don't think he'd be that cunning," Nancy said.

"Then what?"

There was nothing Nancy hated more than admitting she was wrong, but they'd searched everywhere. The leaflets weren't here. They were almost out of time, and they still had no proof of what Lord Evesham was doing. She was so frustrated she wanted to kick something, but everything here was priceless so she restrained herself.

"I think we were probably right the first time," she said. "He's probably keeping them in the stable with the printing machine."

Sidney sank down on the cold stone floor and leaned against a packing case. "So this was all for nothing."

"But we know where the pamphlets are now," said Nancy.

"No, we don't. He could have put them somewhere else."

"I've searched most of the house. And I guess it makes sense that he'd keep all the incriminating evidence in one place."

"So we need to break into the stable," said Sidney.

Nancy stared at her. "Are you mad?"

"I'm game if you are," said Sidney. "Those pamphlets are the only hope we've got of getting anybody to believe what he's doing."

"But how can we break into the stable without being caught? There's no way we could do it in the daytime, and at night he goes in there to print his pamphlets."

"But tomorrow evening he'll be at the dinner," said Sidney. "So the coast should be clear. We could get the pamphlets and then go straight away and drop them on his guests. The boards on the windows must be screwed or nailed to the frames. Bring the tools again, and we'll take off one of the boards, break a window and climb in."

A cold terror crept over Nancy like an icy wind. "That's crazy. You're talking about breaking into Lord Evesham's stables, taking the pamphlets – if they're even there – then storming into his dinner party and scattering them on the guests."

"That was your idea!" said Sidney.

"I know. But I've just realised how ridiculous it

was. Even if we did get that far without being shot –
and we know he carries a gun – as soon as we started
dropping pamphlets he'd get Mr Armitage to throw
us out, and he'd tell his guests we were lunatics. And
who knows what would happen to us afterwards."

"But he's plotting a revolution!" said Sidney. "He's
going to hand over those plans to the Germans on
Friday. And we're probably the only two people in
the world outside his organisation who know what
he's up to. If we don't at least try to defeat him, we're
betraying my brother, and your brother, and every
single person who's fighting the Nazis."

Nancy thought of Jack, and Sidney's poor brother,
and Rosa's brother in an internment camp. Sidney
was right. They had to try.

"But what if we don't find the leaflets?" she said.
"Or what if he explains them away somehow? We
don't actually know what they say, do we? His
name might not be on them. He might say he knows
nothing about them."

Sidney held up a hand. "Wait."

"What?"

"I'm thinking."

Nancy waited, drumming her fingers on a box.

"Stop doing that. I'm trying to work something
out."

Nancy blew out her cheeks in frustration and
drummed her fingers on her skirt instead.

Sidney gazed around the cellar at the hundreds
of neatly labelled boxes containing priceless art
treasures. "What we need is a sort of shield.

Something to stop him throwing us out or shutting us up. Something we can hold in front of us and threaten to destroy if he tries to stop us."

"What do you—" Nancy's eyes followed Sidney's. "Ohhh..."

"What do you think?" asked Sidney. "Would it work?"

"Of course not. It's completely mad. We'd probably go to prison."

"Listen, though. I've got a plan."

As Sidney outlined her idea, Nancy pictured the library, with the balcony running all round it and the door to the balcony from the first-floor landing. A shiver ran through her, a mixture of fear and excitement.

"Do you know what? I think it will work. And I think we should do it."

"So," said Sidney. "Which ones should we take?"

Nancy cast her mind back to the day the art had arrived. "There's a box of vases. About this big." She made the shape of the box with her hands. "He said they were absolutely priceless." She pictured the petrified removal boy carrying the box up the terrace steps. "The label said 'Ming Dynasty, AD 1372'."

"Perfect," said Sidney.

They made their way around the room, using the fading torch beam to scan the label on each box that looked about the right size.

"Here it is!" Nancy said. "'Ming Dynasty, AD 1372'."

She lifted it carefully off the shelf. "Not too heavy

at all," she said.

"We should take another one as well," said Sidney. "There can't be many vases in that box."

Nancy scanned the shelves. "This says 'Qing Dynasty, AD 1740', and it's the right sort of size. Perhaps it's more vases." She tested its weight. "That's fine. Which one do you want to carry?"

"You take the priceless one. You're stronger than me. And you'd better have the torch, too, since yours is more precious. You can hold it in your mouth."

The torchlight was so feeble by now that it was practically useless even for Nancy to see by, and Sidney had to grope her way up without seeing the stair in front of her at all. By the time they reached the top, the beam was so weak that it barely reached the ground.

"I can't climb into the room with the box," whispered Nancy. "I'll put it on the top step. Hold it steady."

"How am I supposed to do that?" hissed Sidney.

"Wedge it with your leg. Just don't let it fall down the stairs."

She set the box precariously on the narrow step. Sidney placed her shin against it while Nancy climbed through the panelling. Sidney handed the boxes through and climbed cautiously into the room.

"We need to remember which panel it was," whispered Nancy, counting the panels up and across as Sidney closed the secret door with a satisfying click. "Two up, four from the left. Remember that."

As they heaved the wardrobe back into place, the

torch battery finally died.

"Blast," whispered Nancy. "We'll just have to be careful."

They inched their way out of the apartment, on high alert for creaking floorboards and toppling ornaments. When they finally emerged into the dimly lit corridor, Nancy felt weak with relief.

"What will we do about the key?" whispered Sidney. "We can't lock the door."

"We'll just have to leave it unlocked. Miss Morris will think she forgot. She'll fret about that all day, poor old fusspot."

"Where shall we put the boxes?"

Nancy's stomach lurched. They hadn't considered this at all.

"What about there?" said Sidney, pointing to a carved oak coffer at the far end of the corridor.

"Let's see what's inside," Nancy said.

The chest contained nothing but woollen blankets full of moth holes.

"Ugh," said Nancy. "Should have been thrown away years ago."

"It's perfect," said Sidney. "We can cover the boxes with blankets." She took hold of a box. Then she said, "Shall we have a peek inside? I'd love to see the vases."

"Are you mad? We need to hide them as fast as we can and get to bed."

"How will we carry them downstairs tomorrow?" asked Sidney. "We'll have to hide them in something. What can be carried up and down stairs without anyone questioning it?"

"Coal buckets," said Nancy. "Housemaids' boxes. But they're not big enough."

"Laundry!" said Sidney. "We can carry laundry bags. Then we can wrap the vases in clothes, to protect them."

Nancy nodded, trying not to look as terrified as she felt. So many things could go wrong with this plan. And the chances of it going right were almost non-existent.

# CHAPTER THIRTY-FOUR

# Both of Us
# or Nothing

"Give the dining table a final polish," said Nancy. "If there's one speck of dust on it when Mr Armitage comes in, there'll be hell to pay."

Sidney's head was throbbing. What with lack of sleep and sheer terror at the thought of what they were planning to do, she had felt sick all day. She'd been so jumpy at lunchtime that she'd knocked the brimming gravy jug over, and Mrs Dawes had called her a useless lazy lump.

She felt like a useless lazy lump. Every bone in her body ached. Her knees were sore from kneeling to wash miles of stone passageways. Her back ached from sweeping acres of carpet with a dustpan and brush. Her wrists and arms hurt from polishing brass doorhandles and candlesticks and bedsteads. Her hands stung, red and rough from the endless scrubbing. It was some distance from the floating about with a pretty feather duster that she'd imagined. How did Nancy stand it?

Despite all that, though, she was grateful for being worked so hard. Pretending to be a servant kept her mind off everything else. Not only the awful visions of George that she had to push away, but also the fact that in a few minutes' time she and Nancy were planning to steal a box of treacherous pamphlets from the stables.

*If they were even there*, thought Sidney. Because what if they weren't at Stanbrook at all? Then this incredibly risky break-in – not to mention last night's expedition – would all have been for nothing.

She jumped as the library door opened. But it was just Mr Armitage, carrying a tray of sparkling silver candlesticks and cutlery. Only the butler was allowed to handle the silver, Nancy had told her.

Mr Armitage didn't even look at the maids. He set the tray on a side table and began inspecting the room, his eyes narrowed. He ran his finger along the top shelf of a bookcase and then peered at his fingertip, turning it this way and that, clearly desperate to find a speck of dust.

The girls stood in silence as he made his way around the room, checking everything from the fringes of the rugs to the folds of the curtains. Eventually he turned to them and said, "What are you idling about for? Go and have your supper."

They nodded and left the room.

"He could at least have said thank you," muttered Sidney.

"Ha!" said Nancy. "You've got a lot to learn about being a housemaid, missy."

They replaced their boxes in the housemaids' closet, and Nancy took two thick floorcloths from a shelf. "Put these in your apron pocket," she said. "Mine's full of tools. Might be useful to have cloths if we're dealing with broken glass."

The smells from the kitchen made Sidney's mouth water, but they could hear Mrs Dawes's raised voice, and Nancy said, "Glad I'm not working in the kitchen tonight. Poor old Florence and Agnes."

They bolted down the cold ham and potatoes that Mrs Dawes had left for them in the servants' hall. Then they headed to the scullery to collect the bucket of household rubbish for the bonfire pile behind the stable block, and the bucket of vegetable peelings for the compost heap. As they climbed the outside steps, Sidney froze. Miss Rutter was leading a line of immaculately turned-out St Olave's girls on to the terrace.

She tugged at Nancy's apron and they retreated to the bottom of the steps. Sidney's heart was racing.

"I forgot! The school's forming a welcoming party for the dinner guests! They're all lining up out there."

"I'll just have to go on my own," said Nancy. She reached for Sidney's bucket, but Sidney held on to it and shook her head vehemently.

"It's both of us or nothing," Sidney said. "You're not breaking into the stable on your own. We have to share the responsibility."

"But what if someone sees you?"

"I'll keep my head down. It'll be fine."

Nancy climbed two steps and peered into the courtyard.

"They're lined up round the edges," she whispered.

"But there's a car coming, so no one will look at us. Stay on the far side of me. I'll shield you."

As they stepped on to the driveway, tyres crunched on the gravel, and the car stopped. A door opened. Sidney couldn't resist turning round to see who was getting out.

It was a chauffeur. He opened the car's back door, and Sidney glimpsed a dull-looking man in a mayoral chain.

She risked a glance up at the schoolgirls. And found herself staring straight into Ginny's eyes.

# CHAPTER THIRTY-FIVE

# Nobody in Site

Dizzy with panic, Sidney whipped her head back round. As she did so, she saw Ginny, her eyes like gobstoppers, nudging Phyllis.

Sidney stumbled after Nancy, who was striding towards the stables. What an idiot she was. What would Ginny and Phyllis do now? Would they tell a teacher? What if they'd made up with Lucinda and they told her?

Should she tell Nancy?

No, definitely not. It would only make her furious. She had suggested doing this by herself and Sidney had insisted on coming. And, after all, Ginny and Phyllis probably wouldn't tell anybody. This might all come to nothing.

Sidney took a deep breath and tried to put the incident out of her mind.

As they walked into the stable yard, they were brought up short by the sight of three gleaming cars. Mr Burford was leaning against a stable door.

Of course. The chauffeurs were parking the cars here! Why hadn't they thought of that? Now they'd have to lurk around until all the cars had arrived and Mr Burford had left the stable yard.

"Evening, girls," Mr Burford said.

"Aren't they lovely cars, Mr B?" said Nancy. "Are there lots more coming?"

"There'll be six altogether," he said.

"And do you have to stay until they've all arrived?"

"Yes, I'm taking the chauffeurs down to the servants' hall for supper. Shouldn't be much longer now, with any luck."

As Sidney took her bucket to the bonfire heap, she heard another car rumble into the stable yard. That must be the one the mayor had just got out of. Her palms started to sweat as Ginny's glance of recognition flashed back into her head. She prayed that Ginny and Phyllis would keep their mouths shut, at least for the next couple of hours. After that, nothing would matter any more.

While Mr Burford took the mayor's chauffeur to the servants' hall, they skulked in the laundry room with their now empty buckets, waiting for the coast to clear.

"I hope nobody's late," said Nancy. "We've got a lot to do."

But the final two cars arrived in quick succession. Mr Burford ushered the last chauffeur indoors, and the girls made their way to the boarded-up stable. The front window was quite low. Nancy took a screwdriver out of her apron pocket and turned her bucket upside down.

"You be lookout," she said, climbing on to the

upturned bucket. "Keep your eyes peeled."

There was no sound or movement in the yard. The horses were out in the paddock and the doors of the other stable block stood open.

Nancy had to work hard to dislodge the first screw, but once she got it moving the rest of it came out easily. She turned to Sidney and scowled.

"You're meant to be keeping a lookout, not looking at me."

As Nancy worked on the other screws, the only sounds in the yard were birdsong and the occasional rustling of an animal in the bushes. The schoolgirls must have filed back indoors.

"Hold the board in place," said Nancy. "This is the last one."

She removed the final screw, and Sidney lifted the board off the window ledge. Nancy tried to push the sash up, but it wouldn't budge.

"I'll have to break a pane," she said. "Then I can undo the catch and slide the window up."

"I'll just have a quick look round," Sidney said. "If anyone hears the glass smashing, we're done for."

She walked all round the stable block, but there was nobody in sight. She nodded to Nancy and winced as Nancy took a hammer from her apron pocket and smashed the windowpane. The noise sounded deafening to Sidney, but nobody came running.

Nancy broke the remaining jagged pieces and reached her hand through the window. As she fumbled with the catch, a terrified voice said, "Sidney? What are you doing?"

# CHAPTER THIRTY-SIX

# Right Before
# Our Eyes

Sidney jerked her head round and found herself staring into Ginny's and Phyllis's pale, shocked faces. Before she could think of anything to say, Nancy jumped off the bucket, snatched a triangular shard of glass from the ground and pointed it a few inches from Ginny's neck.

"Don't breathe a word," she hissed. She jabbed the shard at Phyllis. "You too. Or..." She made a slicing motion.

Phyllis gasped. Ginny raised her hands in terror and took a step backwards.

Nancy glanced at Sidney. "You get the stuff. I'll keep these two covered."

"I really don't think you need—"

"Shut up and get on with it. You two, hands in the air and get behind the stable."

Pointing the glass at their necks, Nancy drove the petrified girls backwards until they were out of sight behind the stable block. Sidney, too stunned to think, climbed on to the upturned bucket and gingerly put her hand through the broken window. The catch was stiff, but eventually she managed to loosen it. She pushed the bottom sash up and then swept the broken glass off the windowsill with a cloth before scrambling up on to the sill and lowering herself into the stable.

The printing press stood right in the middle. A table in the corner was littered with things that were presumably printers' tools and equipment. And in the far corner was a stack of cardboard boxes.

Her heart beating very fast, Sidney undid the string round the top box and opened the flaps. It was full of pamphlets. The headline, in bold black capitals, leapt out at her.

# BRITAIN, ARISE!
## A new dawn for our great country!

She took out a pamphlet. It was a sheet of foolscap paper folded in half to make a four-page leaflet. She read the front page.

The British National League is dedicated to the formation of a united, peaceful and prosperous country for all true British citizens. The British people have for too long been the victims of vicious propaganda spread by a warmongering government, propaganda designed to set loyal British subjects against the great country of Germany, with which we have far more in common than that which divides us.

Herr Hitler, that man of faith and vision, has united

the German people in a common purpose and a common vision, an achievement which our rotten parliamentary democracy has spectacularly failed to achieve. Now it is time for a strong leader to arise and lead our country back to its former greatness.

# PEACE WITH GERMANY!

All Herr Hitler has ever wanted is peace with Britain. But his generous offers of peace have been rejected by our misguided, misinformed, shambolic government.

Now we shall finally have that peace. In the peace deal that the British National League has struck with Herr Hitler, Germany will rule the continent of Europe, and the British Empire will flourish, prosper and grow ever stronger across the rest of the globe. Under the new BNL government, Britain will thrive in an era of harmony and plenty. We, the British people, will finally have the strong and stable government that we truly deserve.

# MAKE BRITAIN GREAT AGAIN!

Sidney's heart was beating painfully hard. This was it! These pamphlets would prove beyond any doubt that Lord Evesham was a fascist who was trying to bring the Nazis to power in Britain. She was so glad she had taken this risk. She had to expose him, whatever happened to her afterwards. She wouldn't be able to live with herself if she didn't.

"Why are you taking so long?" hissed Nancy. "What are you doing?"

"I've found them!" whispered Sidney. "Boxes of them!"

"Bring a stack then, and let's get out of here."

"I'll hand them through the window. We can carry them back in the buckets, with the cloths over the top."

"And if you two little worms move one inch," Sidney heard Nancy murmur, "I'll hunt you down and murder you in your beds. Now, turn your backs and don't look round."

Sidney passed a pile of pamphlets through the window. "Is that enough?"

"Don't be stupid. We need to deluge them with so many that he won't be able to get rid of them."

Sidney passed Nancy enough leaflets to fill both buckets, then she climbed back out of the window. Phyllis and Ginny were still facing the other way.

"Let's stick the board back and get out of here," said Nancy. "We haven't got time to faff around screwing it in."

She climbed on to the upturned bucket and propped the board on the windowsill. Then she turned the bucket the right way up and began filling it with leaflets. "What shall we do with these two?" she asked. "Slit their throats and leave them here?"

"All right, that's enough," said Ginny, turning round to face them. "Sidney, will you just tell us

212

what on earth is going on? I've had enough of being threatened by this lunatic."

"She's not a lunatic," said Sidney. "And we can't tell you anything. It's for your own safety."

"What do you mean?" asked Ginny. "Is this another one of your pranks?" She raised her eyebrows meaningfully at Sidney.

"It's very far from being a prank," said Nancy. "But we're not telling you anything and we're not letting you go until you swear never to breathe a word about this." She picked up the glass and pointed it at their necks again. They recoiled.

"You don't need to threaten them," said Sidney. "I'm sure they won't say anything."

"You don't know what they'll do," said Nancy. "They'll probably go straight to that Lucinda girl and tell her everything."

Phyllis spun round. "We absolutely wouldn't," she retorted.

"Keep your voice down!" hissed Nancy.

"Listen," said Ginny. "We're not sneaks. We saw Sidney and we slipped away and followed you so we could find out what she was doing and whether she was all right. And give her this." From her pocket she took an envelope, addressed to Sidney's parents. "This was on the table where the secretary puts Miss Hathersage's letters for the post. We thought you might want to give your parents your own version of why you were expelled instead of hers."

"Gosh," said Sidney. "Thank you. That was kind."

Ginny shrugged. "And for your information,"

she said to Nancy, "we're not speaking to Lucinda, and she's moved dormitories. We wouldn't snitch anyway, and even if we did, which we wouldn't, the last person in the world we'd snitch to would be her. So how about you tell us what you're up to, and maybe we can help you?"

"We can't tell you anything, and we can't let you help," said Sidney. "It's too dangerous."

"I'd love a bit of danger," said Ginny.

"Me too," said Phyllis.

Nancy gave a scornful laugh. "It's not dangerous like the stupid things you rich people do for thrills. It's not like skiing or falling off your pony. If this goes wrong, we'll be locked up for the rest of our lives. If we don't get killed first."

Ginny and Phyllis were white-faced. "So if you're both risking your lives, it must be very important," said Ginny. "What will happen if it goes right?"

"If it goes right," said Sidney, "we'll stop Lord Evesham and his party from joining with Hitler to turn this country into a fascist dictatorship."

Ginny and Phyllis looked stunned. Nancy looked as though she was about to explode. "What are you doing, Sidney?"

"Lord Evesham?" said Phyllis, her eyes bulging. "Joining with Hitler? That can't be true. How do you know?"

"You must have got things muddled up," said Ginny.

Nancy threw her arms out wide, palms up in an emphatic gesture. "See? They don't believe us any

214

more than anybody else."

"Not until they see the evidence," said Sidney. She took two leaflets out of her bucket and handed them to Ginny and Phyllis. "Have a look at these. Lord Evesham is the leader of a secret organisation called the British National League." She turned to Nancy. "I just found that out from the pamphlets." She quickly explained Lord Evesham's plans to Phyllis and Ginny. Their stunned eyes moved from Sidney to the pamphlets and back again.

"How did you find out about this?" asked Phyllis.

"I'll tell you later. There's no time now." Sidney turned to Nancy. "Listen, I guarantee they won't snitch, and it would really help to have two more people. It would be much more effective, and there'd be safety in numbers too."

"And you don't think it will look a bit odd, two schoolgirls humping laundry bags around?"

"They can hide in the housemaids' closet while we do that bit."

"What if their teachers come looking for them?"

"They won't," said Phyllis, tearing her eyes away from the pamphlet. "We've been given an evening off prep in honour of the dinner, so nobody will be checking on us." She held up the pamphlet. "This is unbelievable. Or it would be if we didn't have the evidence right before our eyes."

"Exactly," said Sidney. "Evidence. Right before your eyes."

"Honestly," said Phyllis, "we want to be involved and we're happy to take the risks. Aren't we, Ginny?"

"Absolutely," said Ginny fiercely, jabbing at the pamphlet. "I can't believe he's been pretending to be a hero all this time, and he's actually a traitor."

"I wish I'd brought my shotgun to school," said Phyllis.

They stared at her, open-mouthed.

"What are you looking so shocked for?" asked Phyllis. "I bet *he* has a gun."

"He does," said Sidney, "but we're not planning to get into a gunfight. We've got a better idea."

"So," said Ginny, "tell us what you're planning and how we can help."

Sidney looked at Nancy, who was still scowling. Nancy shrugged. "Fine. But only because I want them where I can keep an eye on them. And if the bullets start flying, I'm using you two as shields."

Ginny rolled her eyes.

"So what's your plan?" asked Phyllis.

"No questions now," said Sidney. "Let's get you up to the housemaids' closet. You two loiter behind us, so it doesn't look as though we're together."

Sidney and Nancy laid the cloths on top of the pamphlets and made their way towards the house. They left Ginny and Phyllis in the first-floor housemaids' closet with the buckets, and took two empty laundry bags to the big oak coffer outside the dowager's apartment. When they had heaped all the blankets on the floor, Sidney reached in to lift out a packing case.

"What are you doing?" whispered Nancy.

"Taking the vases out, of course."

"Inside the chest, idiot, or there'll be sawdust all over the floor."

The apartment door opened and Miss Morris emerged. Dizzy with terror, Sidney slammed the lid shut. Miss Morris's glance swept over the untidy heap of blankets. She glared at the girls.

"What *are* you doing?"

"Taking these blankets downstairs," said Nancy, gesturing to the laundry bags. "For mending."

She held up a blanket to show Miss Morris the moth holes. The lady's maid gave a tight little nod and headed for the stairs.

Nancy took a chisel out of her apron pocket, and Sidney watched in silence as she deftly levered out the nails in the lid of the packing case and poked around in the tightly packed sawdust.

"Here it is," she whispered, scooping out handfuls of dust into the chest.

Sidney watched, spellbound, as a delicate white circle of porcelain appeared in the sawdust. Nancy scooped out more sawdust and a second porcelain circle appeared on the other side of the box.

She burrowed her hands in and slowly lifted out a large vase. The neck was painted with incredibly detailed flowers and leaves in blue, pink and white on a gold background. The bulbous lower half had a raised fretwork pattern, in the centre of which was a round plaque with two extraordinarily detailed fish painted on it.

"Oh," breathed Sidney. "It's so beautiful. Look at those fish! They've painted every single scale. They must have used a brush with a single hair. Look at the waves, and the patterns in the gold."

"Lovely," said Nancy. "Enjoy it before it gets smashed."

"We can't smash this one. It's too beautiful."

"Yes, you're right," said Nancy. "If it's a choice between saving the country from invasion or keeping this vase in one piece, we should definitely choose the vase."

# CHAPTER THIRTY-SEVEN

# Deadly
# Serious

Nancy and Sidney carried their buckets along the first-floor corridor. Behind them walked Ginny and Phyllis, each cradling a bulging laundry sack.

They arrived at the little door that opened on to the library balcony. Nancy felt sick. This was completely mad. And now that there were more people involved, it was even more likely to go wrong. If it weren't for those snobby little friends of Sidney's judging her, she would have been sorely tempted to call the whole thing off.

A babble of voices came from the library. Nancy grasped the doorknob and nodded to Sidney, who switched off the light in the corridor.

Nancy's heart thumped. Why hadn't she checked that the door didn't squeak?

Still, even if it did, the people in the library wouldn't hear it, not with all the noise they were making. She took a deep breath and very slowly opened the door, just enough for them to slip inside with their precious cargo.

Two shining candelabras, with five tall candles in

each, lit the dining table beneath them. The family silver gleamed in the candlelight. Lord Evesham and his guests stood around the room talking, drinks in their hands. The balcony was in darkness.

Once they were all safely inside, Sidney closed the door and they set the buckets and laundry bags gently on the floor. Nancy loosened the strings of one bag, while Sidney did the other. Nancy held her breath as she eased out the bundles of blankets and placed them on the floor. From the bottom of the bag, she took four candles, four tin saucers and four boxes of matches, all pilfered from the lamp room. She set the saucers in a row on the floor, fixed a candle in each of them and placed a box of matches in each saucer.

Nancy and Sidney carefully unwrapped the vases. Then the girls all picked up a vase and a candle and started crawling along the inner edge of the balcony, keeping close to the bookcases to stay hidden from the dinner guests below.

They crept into position, one on each side of the room, like the four points of a compass. Then Nancy and Sidney crept back for the buckets. Sidney placed half her pamphlets beside Phyllis, and Nancy gave half hers to Ginny.

Once she was sitting cross-legged on the dark balcony, Nancy took a proper look at the dinner guests. By appearing interested and asking Mrs Dawes and Mr Armitage a few questions ("Are all the important people in the county coming?" "Is the lord-lieutenant very old?" "How does somebody become a high sheriff?"), she had found out exactly who would be present and learned some details about each of them. She had written everything down in a little notebook and revised it carefully. Armed with this information, she was able to identify several people in the group below.

The tall one with the moustache was the lord-lieutenant. The short one with the walking stick was the high sheriff. The bulky one with slicked-back dark hair was the chief constable. The stooped one with the thinning hair and the monocle was the Duke of Bowleigh, a prominent member of the House of Lords, who owned a vast estate on the other side of Oxfordshire as well as huge swathes of central London. The very large bald man was the local MP. There were four other Oxfordshire MPs there too, but Nancy wasn't sure which was which. They all looked the same to her: well-fed middle-aged men, highly satisfied with themselves.

Lord Evesham began ushering his guests towards the dinner table, and Mr Armitage left the room, no doubt to fetch the first course. Nancy imagined how fraught the atmosphere in the kitchen would be, as Mrs Dawes seasoned and tasted the soup for the last time. Poor Florence and Agnes.

Just as the guests were seated, the door opened and Mr Armitage appeared, bearing aloft a vast soup tureen as though he were processing up the aisle of Westminster Abbey with the Coronation Crown. Behind him walked Mr Burford, who had been roped in to help wait at table. He had a starched white cloth draped over one arm.

As the men ate their soup, snatches of conversation drifted up to the balcony.

"Impossible to keep staff these days…"

"So I said, if that's how you show your gratitude…"

"Foxes running riot, of course…"

"Absolute pests, no idea of how to behave in the countryside…"

"It's the blackout that's lethal…"

"Couldn't organise a Women's Institute coach trip…"

"Thank God for Churchill. When I think of the cowards begging him to accept Hitler's peace terms…"

"Thing about Churchill is, unlike Chamberlain or Halifax, he understands the nature of the enemy…"

"Better to go down fighting than surrender to Germany…"

"In a nutshell, it's about the defence of freedom against Nazi tyranny…"

"We're doomed unless America enters the war, but Churchill's right, of course: the best way to gain the respect of the Americans is to stand up to Hitler ourselves…"

When the soup bowls were cleared, Nancy's heart began to beat faster. Only one course to go. It had been her idea to wait until after the main course, and now she wished she'd kept her mouth shut.

"If Mum's got to break bad news to Dad," she'd said to Sidney, "she'll always make sure he's had a good meal first."

"Mine too," Sidney had replied.

Mr Armitage reappeared with a huge joint of beef, which was met with so much excitement that Nancy decided they had been right to let them eat their main course first, even though it meant her poor heart was racing and her palms were damp with sweat.

She could just make out Sidney's shadowy figure on the opposite side of the balcony. It was so dark that she couldn't see Phyllis and Ginny at all.

*If those little upstarts mess this up...* she thought.

When the men had finished eating, Mr Armitage and Mr Burford stepped forward to clear the plates. Feeling sick, Nancy fixed her eyes on Sidney, who had insisted on going first.

"You're risking your job by doing this," she had said, "so if it all goes wrong, I need to take the blame."

There was a movement in the shadows, and Sidney's match flared into life. She lit her candle and rose to her feet at the edge of the balcony.

The Duke of Bowleigh glanced up at the light and gave a startled exclamation.

"Good Lord, Evesham, have you arranged some entertainment for us?"

Lord Evesham was deep in conversation with one of the MPs, and didn't hear the duke, but the lord-lieutenant and the high sheriff followed his gaze.

The lord-lieutenant looked astonished. "A ghostly housemaid, by Jove! What is this, Evesham?"

Lord Evesham turned and looked up to see what everybody was staring at. Sidney was holding her candle just below her chin, and a flickering otherworldly light lit her face from beneath.

Lord Evesham leapt from his chair. "What the devil are you playing at? Leave the room immediately."

Sidney stared at him, blank-faced and motionless, exactly as they had planned. If she was terrified, she wasn't showing it, thought Nancy admiringly.

"Who is she, Evesham?" asked the duke.

"How should I know?" said the earl. "Some half-witted servant girl. Go on, get out, before I have you dismissed."

Sidney stood motionless, her eyes fixed on him. "I shall not move," she said, "until you have heard what I have to say."

Lord Evesham's expression changed as he clearly recognised the girl who had tried to break into his stable. Nancy saw fear flash across his face for a second before he said, "Why, you... The audacity!" He turned to his butler. "How did she turn up here in a maid's uniform? Remove her from the room at once."

Mr Armitage nodded. "Yes, my lord." He walked towards the spiral staircase.

"If anybody sets foot on that staircase," said Sidney in clear, ringing tones, "then I shall have no choice but to destroy this." And she set her candle saucer on the wide flat banister and lifted up the Ming vase.

Lord Evesham gasped. "What the...? Where did...? How...?" He turned to Mr Armitage, his face white. "Armitage, did you let this little minx into the strong room?"

Mr Armitage was staring, stupefied, at the priceless vase. He turned to Lord Evesham in a confused daze. "I ... I have no idea how she got hold of it, my lord."

"It was nothing to do with Mr Armitage," said Sidney. "We discovered the secret passage to the strong room."

There was an excited buzz round the table.

"A secret passage?"

"I say, Evesham, how extraordinary."

"Is this some sort of entertainment?"

Lord Evesham's cold voice cut through the rest. "There is no secret passage, and this is clearly a practical joke. I imagine that vase is made of plaster."

"Oh, this vase is genuine," said Sidney. "Ming Dynasty, 1372. At least, that's what it said on the box. And if any of you moves one step closer, or tries to leave the room, or attempts to stop me in any other way, then I'm afraid this vase will have to be sacrificed. As will all the others."

Lord Evesham made a strangled sound. "All the...?"

There was a scratch and a hiss from the other end of the room. The men's heads swivelled as Phyllis's match flared into life. She lit her candle, balanced the saucer on the banister and lifted up the tall porcelain jar.

"Qing Dynasty, 1740," she said, her voice wobbly but clear.

"Good lord, is that Lethbridge's daughter?" said one of the men.

"Can't be, surely."

"By Jove, it is!"

Another scratch and hiss. The men swivelled again.

"Ming Dynasty, 1372," said Ginny, her face illuminated by her candle. She lifted up the matching vase to Sidney's.

Nancy struck her match and the men turned again.

"Qing Dynasty, 1740," she said, as she lit her candle and held up the jar that matched Phyllis's. "And there are plenty more up here," she added in a moment of inspiration.

There was a stunned silence. Then Lord Evesham, his voice trembling with suppressed fury, said, "All right, I have to admit this was an impressive prank. Well done, girls. Now put the vases down and go back to your attics and dormitories."

"Oh, this is no prank," said Nancy. "You need to listen, Lord Evesham. And so do the rest of you. What we are about to tell you is deadly serious."

# CHAPTER THIRTY-EIGHT

# A Pack
# of Lies

An extraordinary hush fell over the room, broken by Lord Evesham's harsh bark of a laugh.

"Oh, come on, gentlemen. You're surely not going to take these hysterical halfwits remotely seriously?"

But the Duke of Bowleigh silenced him with a look. "Let's hear what the girl has to say."

"My name is Nancy Robson," said Nancy. "I'm Lord Evesham's housemaid. I'm sorry to interrupt your dinner, but we have important evidence about his lordship, and we knew nobody would listen unless we did something dramatic."

"Go ahead," said the duke.

"A few weeks ago, I was on my way to the laundry when I heard Lord Evesham and a man called Lonsdale talking in the stables."

"So the hussy's been eavesdropping!" sneered Lord Evesham. "For goodness' sake, gentlemen!"

"Lonsdale, eh?" said the chief constable, suddenly alert. "What did you hear?"

"Lord Evesham said he'd gathered almost all the

information he needed, and he was planning to fly to Ireland on the twenty-first of June to hand it to the German delegation in person."

There were murmurs of consternation from below.

"I remember those were his exact words," said Nancy, "because I wasn't quite sure what they meant at the time."

"Well, of course she wasn't!" said Lord Evesham. "She's a bally skivvy!" He turned to his guests. "In case you've forgotten, gentlemen, I'm engaged in highly sensitive work at the Air Ministry. Those of us at the very highest levels are involved in matters of an extremely delicate nature, the exact content of which I can't reveal for obvious reasons."

"That's what Mr Armitage said when I reported it to him," said Nancy.

She glanced at Mr Armitage, who was gazing at her in horror.

Now Lord Evesham looked horrified. "Reported it! You presumptuous…" He took a breath and turned to his guests again. "As you can see, gentlemen, she's put two and two together and made fifty, as servants always do. And we've given them the vote! No wonder this country's going to the dogs. We're run by housemaids and road sweepers, and they call it democracy."

Sidney stood up, balancing the vase on the balcony rail in front of her. "I'm a pupil at St Olave's," she said. "I'll explain about the housemaid's uniform later. I was in the garden a couple of weeks ago when

I overheard a conversation between Lord Evesham and Dorothy Taylor, the racing driver."

The chief constable and one of the MPs exchanged glances.

"Eavesdropping again!" said Lord Evesham. "I don't know why you're giving this rot the time of day."

"They were discussing bringing something secretly to the stables here at midnight," Sidney continued. "It sounded intriguing, and since my dormitory overlooks the stables, I decided to stay up and watch from the window. Dorothy Taylor arrived in a van and they unloaded a large object into a stable, which Lord Evesham locked."

The men looked at Lord Evesham curiously. His face was slightly flushed as he said, "I apologise, gentlemen, for wasting your time with this irrelevant drivel. Miss Taylor and I share an interest in cars, and she was delivering some new parts for me."

"At midnight?" said the chief constable.

"She's a busy woman," said Lord Evesham with an attempt at a chuckle. But nobody else laughed.

"A week or so later," said Sidney, "we decided to play a prank. We hid under the dust sheets that cover the statues in the Long Gallery, to scare the other girls in my dorm."

Phyllis gasped. She turned to Sidney, open-mouthed. Ginny raised her eyebrows at Sidney with a knowing look.

Lord Evesham gave a triumphant exclamation. "You see! A schoolgirl prank. Exactly as I said.

Why the devil are you paying any attention to these children?"

"While we were hiding," said Nancy, "Lord Evesham walked in, with Dorothy Taylor. He said their organisation now had members in every government department, including the War Cabinet. He also said the main body of the police was with them, though there was a bad patch higher up, including the local chief constable."

Everybody's eyes turned to the chief constable. He looked at Lord Evesham, who said, "Oh, for goodness' sake! I'm not listening to another word of this nonsense."

He stepped towards the staircase. Nancy took one hand off her vase, which was balanced on the balcony rail. Lord Evesham gasped and froze. A glorious feeling of power surged through Nancy.

"Sorry," she said. "You're making me nervous, and when I get nervous, my hands shake. It would probably be better if you stayed where you were. I'd feel terrible if the vase crashed to the floor."

Lord Evesham went purple with rage, but he stayed where he was.

"The most shocking thing," said Nancy, "was when Lord Evesham said he was pretty confident that the head of the armed forces, General Steel, would join their revolution."

"By Jove! Steel?" said one of the MPs. "I didn't think there was any truth in those rumours."

"Of course there's no truth in them!" said Lord Evesham, practically hopping with irritation. "This is all a pack of lies, that's obvious."

"His lordship said our system of government is rotten to the core," said Nancy, "and we need a bloody revolution. He said the battle would be over very quickly because his organisation has members in the LDV and the forces to disrupt the British defences."

The members of the rotten British government stared at Lord Evesham in speechless shock. Even by candlelight, Nancy could see his face had turned pale.

"Oh, come on," said the high sheriff. "You're surely inventing all this?"

"Of course they're inventing it!" said Lord Evesham. "You can't be gullible enough to give the slightest credence to some ridiculous story they've no doubt concocted as a dare."

"They said the Air Force needed to be destroyed before Hitler could invade," said Sidney. "Dorothy Taylor offered to bomb more aircraft factories like she had bombed the Spitfire factory here."

"What?" cried the high sheriff. But Nancy noticed that the chief constable looked interested rather than surprised.

"Lord Evesham said he was flying to Ireland to personally give the Germans the plans of every airfield and aircraft factory in the country," said Sidney.

The room erupted into startled exclamations.

"It might interest you to know, gentlemen," said Lord Evesham, looking far more confident now, "that this girl has been proven to be mentally unstable. Her headmistress has recommended to her parents that she be institutionalised. She has a grudge against me because I caught her snooping around the stable block and she was expelled as a consequence. Just look at her, for goodness' sake! Expelled from school, and yet she's come back disguised as a housemaid."

The chief constable gave Sidney a hard look. "Is this true?"

Nancy saw that Sidney's hands were trembling.

"It's true I was expelled," she said. Her voice was a little shaky but she kept steady eye contact with the men below. "Lord Evesham did catch me snooping around the stables. I was trying to find out what he'd smuggled in there. But I'm not mentally unsound. He said that because I know too much, and he wants me locked up in an institution. I swapped places with the new housemaid so I could let you all know he's a traitor."

"Tell me this, young lady," said the high sheriff. "If you really did hear all you claim to have heard, then you must have known it was your duty to report it. So why on earth have you kept quiet until now?"

"We haven't," said Sidney. "I reported it to the headmistress and Nancy reported it to Mr Armitage, as she told you. Neither of them believed us. Nancy telephoned the police, but they didn't believe her either. So we came up with this plan instead, because we knew you were the most important people in the county, and we hoped you might listen to us."

"It's a dramatic story, I'll give you that," said the high sheriff. "You've got good imaginations and I suppose you read the newspapers or listen to the wireless, so you know a few names. But it's clearly just a story. All you've done is report conversations that you claim to have overheard. You haven't presented us with a single shred of evidence."

"Exactly!" expostulated Lord Evesham. "Thank heaven for somebody talking a bit of sense! The whole thing's made up from beginning to end. It's laughable really, how gullible some of you are. Listening to these half-witted females with your jaws dropping like goldfish. And your behaviour," he said, jabbing his finger at the girls, "is an absolute disgrace. I've never heard anything like it in my life. Armitage, get rid of them, for pity's sake."

Mr Armitage took a step towards the spiral staircase. All four girls balanced their vases precariously on the balcony rail and took one hand away. Nancy lifted her vase into the air.

"Stop!" screeched Lord Evesham.

Nancy balanced the vase back on the rail, but she only kept one hand on it.

"Girls," said Lord Evesham in a softer tone and with an attempt at a smile. "Whatever this little piece of play-acting was, you've carried it out extremely effectively. Well done, all of you. Now put the vases down very, very carefully, and if there's no damage to them, then we'll forget all about it, eh? But if any harm comes to them, then I'm afraid that's called criminal damage, and you'll be put in prison for a very long time. Do you understand?"

"Absolutely," said Nancy. "Before we leave, though, there is just one more thing we thought we should mention."

# CHAPTER THIRTY-NINE

# Fire!

Sidney felt an unnatural hush descend on the room. Perhaps it was the calm confidence in Nancy's voice. She seemed completely unruffled by Lord Evesham's threats. She actually looked as though she was enjoying herself.

"Dorothy Taylor mentioned something interesting," said Nancy. "She asked Lord Evesham about his printing press. He said he had several thousand pamphlets printed, ready to drop from aeroplanes as soon as the revolution happened."

"What fantastical nonsense!" scoffed Lord Evesham.

"Oh, you say it's nonsense?" asked Nancy.

"Of course it is."

"That's interesting." Nancy paused and looked round the assembled company. "We found the printing press. That's what they were smuggling into the stable."

A look of panic crossed Lord Evesham's face, but he composed himself immediately.

"For goodness' sake," he said, "how much longer

are you going to pay attention to these ridiculous lies?"

"We can show you if you'd like to see it," Sidney told the men.

"Of all the cheek!" exploded Lord Evesham. "My guests are here to eat a good dinner, not be taken on a wild goose chase around the grounds."

"We'll show you with pleasure," said Nancy. "But just before you see it, here are some of the pamphlets he's been printing. We found them in the stable. There are lots more boxes there, but we brought over a few to show you."

The girls set down their vases and picked up their piles of pamphlets. Sidney tossed a handful into the air as though she were throwing confetti at a wedding. Phyllis hurled two handfuls into the middle of the room. Ginny threw hers so enthusiastically that they hit the ceiling.

From all four sides of the balcony, a steady stream of pamphlets whirled and fluttered to the floor. Lord Evesham scrambled to pick them up, but there were far too many, and they continued to rain down. Some hit the guests on the head. Some landed on the dining table and were soaked in gravy. The lord-lieutenant, gazing up in astonishment, had a pamphlet fall squarely on his face. As they showered down, the men snatched them up and scanned them eagerly. Exclamations of horror and outrage bubbled up around the room, the noise swelling and rising as the pamphlets continued to land. The chief constable said something to Mr Burford, who nodded and left the room.

"Fakes!" cried Lord Evesham, gesticulating wildly. "They're fakes. They've printed them themselves. I've never seen them before!" His voice was growing higher and more desperate.

The chief constable strode to the foot of the spiral staircase. "Will one of you show me this printing press?" he called.

"I will," said Nancy immediately. "Guard my vase, Phyllis."

As Nancy ran down the spiral staircase, Sidney saw Lord Evesham hurrying towards the door.

"Stop him!" she yelled. "He's trying to escape!"

The duke glanced round, saw the earl making for the door and stepped in front of him. Lord Evesham grabbed his shoulders and shoved him aside.

"I say, steady on," said the high sheriff.

Lord Evesham made it to the door, but the chief constable had placed himself in front of it like a guard dog. Lord Evesham reached out to grab the handle and the chief constable grasped his wrist in a firm grip.

"I wouldn't try anything on if I were you, sir," he said.

Lord Evesham turned and glanced at the spiral staircase, but one of the MPs saw the glance and blocked the stairs.

"Keep a firm hold of him," said the chief constable to the MPs. "I'm going to have a look at this printing press."

"If he tries to leave," cried Sidney, "we'll smash the vases to smithereens."

What a wonderful word "smithereens" was. She'd never said it aloud before.

"Smithereens!" she shouted again, lifting her vase high in the air.

"Put that down!" screeched Lord Evesham, trying to shake off the men. "I'll have you strung up, you pack of hooligans!"

The MPs kept a firm grip on his arms and steered him away from the door. Nancy elbowed her way through the throng to the chief constable's side. But as they reached the door, a voice from outside the room screamed, "Fire!"

Everybody froze. The chief constable flung the door open. And Lucinda Gore-Withers burst into the room.

"Fire!" she panted. "Fire in the stables!"

Sidney almost dropped her vase in astonishment. Lucinda's face was smeared with soot. There were flakes of ash in her dishevelled hair.

"Get your hands off me!" Lord Evesham barked at his captors. "Don't you hear, my stables are on fire!"

"It's all right, your lordship!" Lucinda cried over the babble of voices. "I put the fire out. I ran to the other stables and grabbed the horses' water buckets and threw them over the flames, and I found a hose and used that too."

"Excellent quick thinking, young lady," said the chief constable. "That's most impressive."

Lucinda beamed with pride.

"Get off me, you imbeciles!" spat Lord Evesham

238

to the MPs.

"Don't worry, your lordship," said Lucinda. "I told the mistresses and they've gone to check that everything's all right. The horses are safe: they were all out in the field, and the fire was in a disused stable anyway. There were just boxes in there, and some sort of machine. But you'll never believe who started the fire, your lordship! I wouldn't believe it myself, but I saw her with my own eyes."

The chief constable looked extremely interested. "Who did you see?"

"Well," said Lucinda, clearly savouring her moment in the spotlight, "I went out to see your hunter, your lordship – such a beautiful horse, and he and I have formed a very strong connection. And there, running out of the disused stable, was Dorothy Taylor! The racing-car driver! I recognised her from the newspapers. She was carrying a petrol can, and when she saw me she threw the can into the bushes, jumped on to her motorcycle and rode away. Isn't that extraordinary? She must be completely mad, mustn't she?"

"I should say so," said the lord-lieutenant.

Sidney tried to make sense of this dramatic news. Dorothy Taylor must have come to print more pamphlets, seen the broken window and the opened boxes, realised the printing press had been discovered, and decided to destroy the evidence by burning down the stable.

"You've done a terrific job, young lady," said the chief constable. "Well done."

Lucinda tried to look modest. "I couldn't save most of the boxes, but I saved the machine. And I managed to drag one of the boxes away before it caught fire."

"You idiot!" spat Lord Evesham. He lunged towards Lucinda, but the men pulled him back. "You little fool! You've ruined everything!"

Lucinda stumbled backwards, the colour draining from her face. "I ... I did the best I could, your lordship. I think ... I mean, it will need repairing, but you'll be able to get it working again."

"Thank you, Lucinda," said Sidney. "You've been wonderful. Dorothy Taylor nearly ruined everything, but you saved the day. We couldn't have done it without you."

Lucinda turned. Her mouth dropped open as she saw Sidney. For the first time, she seemed to take in the chaos around her: the abandoned dinner; the litter of pamphlets; Lord Evesham desperately trying to free himself from the grip of several men. She stared at Sidney in her maid's uniform, her face clouded with confusion.

"Wh-what...? How...?"

The chief constable stepped over to the struggling peer.

"Lord Evesham," he said. "I am arresting you on suspicion of treachery."

"This is an outrage!" said Lord Evesham. "Get your filthy hands off me, all of you."

"I've had a call put through to the police station," said the chief constable to the men restraining Lord

Evesham. "Officers will be arriving shortly to take him away, but I'd be grateful if you could keep hold of him in the meantime."

"With pleasure," said an MP.

"Have courage, your lordship," said Lucinda, hurrying over to him. "There's obviously been a terrible misunderstanding, but I will investigate, and I shan't rest until you're freed."

"Get away, you little fool," snapped Lord Evesham.

Lucinda backed away like a wounded animal. Sidney almost felt sorry for her.

The chief constable shifted his gaze to the balcony. "Come down, girls, would you?"

They put down their vases. Sidney's legs felt weak and shaky, and she leaned heavily on the banister as they walked down the spiral staircase.

"Congratulations, all of you," said the chief constable. "That was quite a coup you pulled off there."

"It was Sidney and Nancy's idea," said Phyllis. "We only joined in at the last minute."

"I'll have to ask you to come down to the station tomorrow and give me a bit more information. I'll be in touch with the butler – and your headmistress, I suppose?" he said to Ginny and Phyllis.

As he turned his attention back to Lord Evesham, Nancy grinned at Sidney. "We did it!"

Sidney smiled. "I can't believe he's actually been arrested."

As she said the words, the tension began to leave her body. She felt her shoulders sink and her breathing come more easily. He had been arrested!

Somebody knocked at the door. Mr Armitage, who had been standing against the wall as though in a trance, seemed to resurface at the sound of the knock. Here, at last, was something that he knew how to respond to. He stood up tall, pushed his shoulders back and opened the door.

In the doorway stood Miss Hathersage, her lips pursed and her face tense. Her eyebrows shot up at the sight of the overturned chairs, the trampled pamphlets, and the gravy congealing on uncleared plates. Her eyes travelled over the mayhem until they located her three uniformed pupils. Sidney, in her maid's uniform, seemed to be invisible to her.

The chief constable walked over to greet the headmistress. Mr Armitage stepped forward. "Miss Hathersage, may I introduce Chief Constable Peaty of the Oxfordshire Constabulary. Chief Constable, Miss Millicent Hathersage, headmistress of St Olave's School."

"Delighted to meet you, ma'am," said the chief constable, offering his hand.

Miss Hathersage shook it automatically, though clearly in some distress. "Chief Constable, I must apologise for the atrocious behaviour of my pupils. I was informed that Lucinda Gore-Withers was seen running towards this room. I can only assume she was in shock after discovering the fire. I'm afraid I have no idea," she said with a cold glance at the two girls, "what Virginia and Phyllis are doing here."

"Being extremely brave and resourceful, I'm

happy to say," said the chief constable. "You can be very proud of them, ma'am. And I think this is one of your pupils too."

Miss Hathersage's eyes fell on Sidney and her head jerked in startled recognition.

"I'm sorry, miss, I don't know your name," the chief constable said.

"Sidney Dashworth, sir."

"Thank you. Well," he said to Miss Hathersage, whose face was a picture of fury, "Miss Dashworth has done herself and the school great credit, and I'm sure you'll want to congratulate her. Very well done, Sidney."

The chief constable shook her hand and then looked expectantly at the headmistress.

"Congratulations, Sidney," said Miss Hathersage through tightly pursed lips.

The door opened and Mr Burford ushered in two policemen. The chief constable said a few words to them, and they nodded and walked over to the group round Lord Evesham. The MPs stepped aside and the policemen handcuffed Lord Evesham and led him out of the room. Lord Evesham kept his head to the ground and said nothing. Lucinda and Miss Hathersage watched, dumbfounded.

As the chief constable passed Lucinda, he said, "Great work there, young lady. Your quick thinking made sure he couldn't destroy the evidence."

Lucinda opened her mouth, but no words came out. The MPs, released from their guard duties, came over to congratulate the girls. But Mr Burford got there first.

"That was quite something," he said to Nancy. "Your parents will be very proud. Pretty extraordinary, wasn't it, Mr Armitage?"

"Certainly," said Mr Armitage in a voice almost as choked as Miss Hathersage's. He gave a stiff little nod. "Congratulations, Nancy."

Nancy gave a wide, cheerful grin. "Thank you, Mr A. I bet you wish you'd believed me now, don't you?"

Mr Armitage coughed and turned away.

"Bet you wish you'd believed Sidney too, don't you, Headmistress?" said Nancy.

Miss Hathersage pretended she hadn't heard.

"By the way, Mr A," said Nancy, "I shall be handing in my notice. There's just something I need to return first." And she took the two SPS notebooks out of her apron pocket.

# CHAPTER FORTY

## Last Day
## of Term

The courtyard was a jumbled mass of school trunks, overnight bags, tennis racquets, abandoned books and mislaid gym shoes. Girls zigzagged between the objects, chattering, laughing, saying their goodbyes and promising to write or visit in the holidays.

Miss Newsom strode purposefully through the chaos, examining items for name tapes and reuniting them with their owners. Miss Rutter hovered by the terrace steps, consulting a clipboard as trunks were loaded into the coaches that would take the girls to the station. Girls who lived closer, or whose parents had saved enough of their petrol ration to come by car, were anxiously scanning the drive for approaching vehicles.

"You will come and stay, won't you?" Sidney pleaded to Ginny and Phyllis, as they sat on the lawn. "I don't think I can bear it otherwise." She was dreading going home, where every familiar thing would be a constant reminder of George's absence.

"Of course I will," said Ginny. "I said I would."

"I'd love to," said Phyllis, "but I can't leave my

245

animals. Why don't you come to Scotland and meet Dusty and Pepper?"

"Goodness, look at that car," said Ginny, as an enormous, highly polished Bentley made its stately way up the drive. "And a uniformed chauffeur."

Sidney saw Lucinda pick up her overnight bag and walk towards the car. "Of course," she said, motioning to the others.

"Did you hear she's moving to a different school next term?" said Phyllis.

"Really?" said Sidney. "How do you know?"

"Amanda told me. Apparently there aren't enough girls from good families at St Olave's. Lucinda said her parents don't want her associating with the wrong sort of people."

Sidney laughed. "How lovely. It will be so much nicer without her."

She watched as the chauffeur loaded Lucinda's luggage into the boot. "Where's she spending the summer? Her parents are in India, aren't they?"

"Yes, she hasn't seen them for years," said Ginny. "She spends holidays with relatives. I think she's going to her grandmother's this time."

As the car set off down the drive, Sidney looked at the lonely figure in the back seat and, to her surprise, felt a twinge of sympathy for Lucinda. Perhaps she would be able to make a fresh start at her new school.

"Girls with surnames A to M, line up for the first coach, please," called Miss Rutter.

"Back in a minute," said Sidney to the others, and before they could ask questions, she hurried into the house.

From the open window of the dowager's apartment, Nancy saw Ginny and Phyllis queuing for the coaches. Laughter and chatter floated up from the courtyard.

"Come and drink your tea, Margaret, before it gets cold," said the dowager. "And look, Cook has sent up the most delicious biscuits."

Nancy joined her on the sofa, where the dowager had her SPS notebook open on her lap. She hadn't let it out of her sight since Nancy had returned it to her.

There was a knock at the door. Opening it, Nancy was surprised to see Sidney.

"I know we exchanged addresses yesterday," Sidney said, "but I just wanted to say goodbye properly."

"Come in," said Nancy. "My lady, may I introduce my friend Sidney from St Olave's."

The dowager smiled a vague, rather nervous smile. She didn't seem to understand.

"It must be nice to spend more time in here," said Sidney, looking around the pretty apartment.

"It certainly beats cleaning. Course, there's less cleaning to do, what with his lordship being in prison."

They grinned at each other. "And Dorothy Taylor too," said Sidney. "I still can't quite believe we did that, can you? It's such a shame we have to keep it secret."

"It's fun to think about, though," said Nancy.

"And at least we can talk about it with each other. You will write, won't you? And you'll still be here when I come back next term?"

"For the time being, yes. I changed my mind when Mr Armitage offered me a pay rise. And he gave me my copy of *Jane Eyre* back. I have to say it's nice getting a bit more respect. And her ladyship likes having me here. I read aloud to her a lot, and she doesn't mind what I read, so I choose whatever I like from the library." She indicated a book on the table.

Sidney read the title. "*The Odyssey* by Homer? You're reading Latin for fun?"

"It's Greek," said Nancy. "But translated into English. It's really good. As soon as I'm old enough, though, I'm going to join the ATS and train as a mechanic. And after this war is over, I want to be an engineer, like Amy Johnson or Beatrice Shilling. I've written to the Women's Engineering Society for advice on what to study, so I can get a head start. No getting married and slaving for some man for me."

"I think I'd quite like to get married," said Sidney. "But I'd like to write books too. Detective stories." She walked to the window and gazed out at the scene in the courtyard. "Rosa's coming back as well, isn't she?"

"Yes, on Monday. Though my parents love her so much, I think they'd have liked her to stay forever. She's hoping her brother might be released soon too, after the outcry in the papers about all the innocent people being interned."

"Oh!" cried Sidney, staring at a car coming slowly

up the drive. "There's my parents! How strange, I thought I was going by train. There must have been a muddle."

Looking at the car, Sidney felt sick with dread at the thought of the endless days ahead, all three of them lost in their grief. At least Ginny's visit would be a distraction.

"I'd better go down," she said. "Can you come and meet them?"

"You go," said Nancy. "I'll pop down in a minute if her ladyship can spare me."

Sidney reached the courtyard as the car stopped on the gravel.

"Sidney Dashworth," said Miss Rutter, tapping her clipboard with a pencil. "Where have you been? You've kept the whole coach waiting."

"I'm sorry, madam," said Sidney. "But my parents have come by car."

Miss Rutter tutted. "They really should have informed me of the change of plan. Now your trunk will have to be unloaded as well." She turned away with a sigh. "Miss Newsom, can you assemble the girls for the second coach, please?"

Miss Newsom's whistle blew deafeningly close to Sidney's ear. "All girls with surnames N to Z, line up now," she called.

Girls surged across the courtyard as the first coach pulled away, with Ginny and Phyllis waving frantically from a window. Sidney waved back and pointed to her parents' car to reassure them. She would write to them both tomorrow.

Even from across the courtyard, she could see that her father looked surprisingly cheerful as he got out of the car. She felt a surge of anger. What did he have to be cheerful about?

Through the crowd of pupils, she saw him open the passenger door for her mother. Then he opened the back door on the passenger side. Sidney frowned. Who had they brought with them?

The stranger was facing away from her, but Sidney could tell it was an old man, from the slow, careful way he got out, as though all his joints were stiff. He gradually straightened up, leaning on a crutch, and then he turned his face in her direction.

For a second, she stood rooted to the spot, unable to believe her eyes. Then he gave her a lopsided grin, and a surge of pure joy propelled her across the courtyard.

"George! Oh, George!"

Heads turned as she raced towards the drive, weaving between groups of girls, tripping over bags and banging into elbows.

"George! Oh, George, you're back!"

Leaping over a bag of tennis balls, she flew down the steps and threw her arms round her laughing brother.

"Steady on, sis," he said in that warm familiar voice. "I'm not as young as I was, you know."

"Oh, George, it's really you! You're alive! You've come back!"

He had a vivid red burn all down one side of his face, and his left foot was in plaster. He looked older and thinner, altered in some irrevocable way. But he was George. He was her brother. And he was home.

On the South Lawn, tea tables had been set up in front of the Long Gallery for parents to refresh themselves before the drive back home. While their parents discussed traffic problems and fuel shortages, Sidney and George walked around the garden.

"I'm like an elderly snail, I'm afraid," said George, "but I need to keep moving, or I'll seize up completely."

"Go as slowly as you like," said Sidney. "We're in no hurry."

George didn't want to talk much about his experiences over the last few weeks, but he gave his sister a brief summary. When his plane went up in flames, he had managed to bail out by parachute over the German lines. Because he was in enemy territory, he had hidden in a ditch until it grew dark, and then he had crept out and walked all night. His progress was slow because he had a very sore foot and had to use a stick. Luckily he had come to a farm, where the French family had given him food. They were too frightened to help him further, in case they were punished by the occupying forces, so for several days he was forced to hide by day and limp on by night, until finally he came across a British patrol who took him to a field hospital. There his foot, which turned out to be broken, was set in plaster, and his burns treated, and eventually he was evacuated back to England.

"I finally made it home yesterday," he said. "The parents wanted to telephone you with the news, but I thought it would be more fun to give you a surprise."

"It's the best surprise in the world," Sidney said. Then she took a breath, crossed her fingers and asked the question that had been playing insistently in her head while he had been talking. "So is that it for you now? Is that the end of the flying?"

"Certainly not," he replied. "If Douglas Bader can fly with two artificial legs, I should hope I'll be all right with a few knocks and scars. I'll be back in my Spitfire as soon as they let me. But that's quite enough about me. Tell me what you've been up to."

"Well," said Sidney, pointing into the Long Gallery, "under that dust sheet, there's a statue of Cupid."

So she told her brother all about Nancy and the statue prank. Well, almost all. She finished at the point where the others had run from the room in hysterics. The rest would have to wait.

"I say," said George, leaning on his crutch and looking along the path, "is that the girl you played the prank with? Or are there several red-haired maids here?"

"Nancy!" called Sidney, running to meet her friend. "Oh, Nancy, the most amazing thing's happened!"

"I saw from upstairs!" beamed Nancy. "I saw him getting out of the car, and I knew it must be your brother, and I was so happy I burst into tears."

"Isn't it incredible? I feel like I'm floating on air. Come and meet him." She took Nancy's arm and hurried her across the lawn.

"George," she said, "this is my friend Nancy."

"Very pleased to meet you, George," said Nancy.

George grinned as he shook her hand. "Ah, the famous Nancy. Last seen waving her arms about and moaning under a dust sheet."

Nancy gave Sidney an incredulous look. "You've told him that already?"

"Well, it's a darn good story," said George.

"It is," said Nancy. Then her eyes opened wide, and she grabbed Sidney's arm. "*That's* what you should write, Sidney. That should be your first book. Not with our real names, of course. Write it as a story."

"The statue prank?" said Sidney.

"All of it," said Nancy. "Right from the beginning, when we both arrived. And finishing here, with the happy ending, like all stories should."

"I'm not sure this is really the ending," said Sidney, thinking about George going back up in his Spitfire, and the long war that surely lay ahead of them.

"Well, it's a good place to finish the story," said Nancy.

"Yes," said Sidney, gazing at the beautiful gardens and the green fields beyond, on this perfect, cloudless summer's day. "Yes, I think it is."

# Author's Note

The events in this story are fictional, but they are based on the fact that some British aristocrats were involved in treacherous activities during the Second World War. Many of these are detailed in the book *Hitler's British Traitors* by Tim Tate, which uses files released to the National Archives by MI5, the Home Office and the Treasury between the years 2000 and 2017. Most of these activities were conducted in secret, and few of the aristocratic men and women involved were ever prosecuted. Their wealth and powerful connections protected them from the punishments given to less well-connected traitors.

# Acknowledgements

I am so lucky to work with the amazing team at Nosy Crow. Massive thanks to Catherine Stokes, Rebecca Mason, Hannah Kettle, Hannah Prutton, Kellie Balseiro, Xeni Soteriou, Jono Ganz and the wonderful Sales, Marketing and Publicity teams. I am so grateful for all the work you do to send my books out into the world.

Thank you so much to Ray Tierney for the fantastic cover design, and to David Dean for the amazing cover illustration. I can't express how much I love this cover!

I am very grateful to Jenny Glencross for such a helpful and encouraging line edit, and to Hazel Cotton and Jennie Roman for invaluable copy edits at different stages of the process. Thank you very much to Nicki Lampon and Laura Roberts for your eagle-eyed proof reading.

Thanks beyond measure to my superb and wonderful editor, Kirsty Stansfield. Thank you for your enthusiasm for the initial idea, your insightful comments and brilliant suggestions at every stage, your patience in reading more drafts than I care to remember, and your constant encouragement throughout the process. I couldn't have done it without you.

Thank you to all the wonderful members of my Creative Writing Club over the past eight years, and especially to long-standing members Amelia, Daisy,

Fleur, Hannah, Maddie and Mairi. Thank you for sharing your ideas and your work so generously, and for being such a mutually supportive and endlessly creative group of people.

Huge thanks to my amazing children, Freddy and Dorothea, for your feedback on the story at various stages. However painful it sometimes was to hear, it always helped to make the book better!

And, as always, infinite thanks to my husband, Oliver, for your thoughtful comments on the work in progress and most of all for your constant and unstinting support.

Turn the page for a sneak peek at another
brilliant book by Helen Peters!

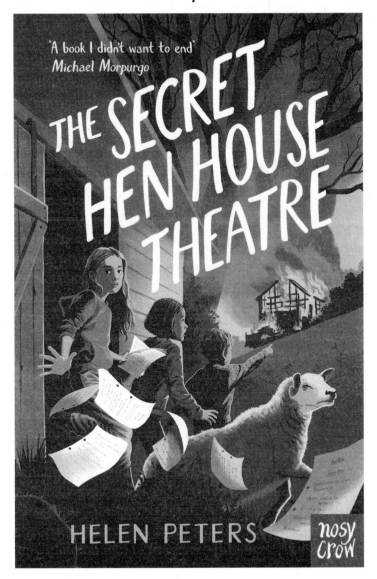

"A book I didn't want to end"
Michael Morpurgo

THE SECRET HEN HOUSE THEATRE

HELEN PETERS

nosy crow

# CHAPTER ONE

# The Stranger

BANG, BANG, BANG!

Somebody was trying to smash the scullery door down.

Hannah sat cross-legged on her bedroom floor, hunched over a piece of paper, her pen racing across the page. Even inside the farmhouse her breath came out in white trails, and the cold sneaked its way right through her woolly hat and three jumpers.

BANG, BANG, BANG!

Her right hand didn't leave the page as she glanced at her watch. Five to two. But it couldn't be Lottie. She never knocked. She just walked right in and yelled up the stairs.

One of the others could get it for once. She had to finish this by two o'clock.

BANG, BANG, BANG!

"Will someone answer that blasted door!" shouted her dad from the farm office.

There! Finished at last. Hannah wrote "THE END" in large capital letters. This play would win the competition, she just knew it.

BANG, BANG, BANG!

"Hannah!" called Dad.

"Oh, *OK*." Hannah slid her mother's copy of *Putting On a Play* under her bed and scrambled to her feet. She must remember to put that back in Mum's bookcase later.

"If it's for me, tell them I'm not in," Dad called as she passed his office door. "And get the others ready. There's a pig wants bringing up from the Anthill Field."

Hannah ran down the splintered back stairs, script in hand, ducking the cobwebs that hung from the crumbling ceiling. Her little brother Sam was already at the door, fumbling with the latch.

"It's stuck again," he said.

"I'll get it, Sammy," said Hannah. Sam moved aside. His laces were undone and his shoes were on the wrong feet.

BANG, BANG, BANG!

As Hannah wrestled with the battered latch, her eight-year-old sister Jo came through from the kitchen, a flat cap pulled down over her curls. A ginger guinea pig nestled into her left arm, nibbling a cabbage leaf.

"Who's come?" she asked.

The latch shot up. Sam glued himself to Hannah's side as she opened the door. Jo hovered by the stairs.

Looming in the doorway, stamping his feet against the cold, was a stocky man with a red face and a puffed-out chest. He looked like an irate turkey. His shiny dark hair was greased down on his head and he grasped a clipboard with his thick red fingers.

He stared at the children. "Flipping heck," he muttered. His breath hung in the air.

What's wrong with him? thought Hannah. She looked round but there was nothing, only the three of them in their holey jumpers and torn jeans. Had he never seen farm clothes before?

Click, clack, click, clack.

They all turned. At the top of the steep staircase, in a white minidress and red stilettos several sizes too big for her, stood ten-year-old Martha, one hand on her hip and her chin in the air.

"Martha," said Hannah, "you'll die of pneumonia. Go and get changed. And take Mum's shoes off. Dad'll go ballistic."

"Oh, shut up," said Martha. "You're just jealous cos I look like a model."

The man raised his eyebrows. Martha tottered down the stairs and pushed past Jo to get a good look at him.

"I'm looking for –" The man glanced at the clipboard. "Clayhill Farm."

They said nothing.

"Is this Clayhill Farm?" he asked, louder now. "There's no sign."

"The sign blew down," said Sam.

Hannah noticed a very new, very big, very shiny black BMW parked in the farmyard. At least, the top half was shiny. The bottom half was plastered in mud, like every vehicle that came up the farm track.

"In the records, it says it's a working farm," he said.

"It is," said Hannah. Was he really thick or something? And who was he anyway, coming up here on a Sunday afternoon asking nosy questions?

"Really? Then what's all this junk lying around for?" He flicked his hand around the yard. At the horse ploughs half buried in grass, the collapsed combine harvester rusting in the mud by the pigsties, the old doors, oil stoves and tangled barbed wire heaped up outside the house. "I mean, what's with that old rust bucket?" He pointed towards the tractor shed where Dad's vintage tractor stood. "What is it – an engine from the Age of Steam?"

"It's Daddy's Field Marshall," said Sam proudly. "It's really old."

"Huh. You don't say."

Sam turned puzzled eyes to Hannah, and Hannah felt her cheeks flushing. How dare he be rude to Sam? And how ignorant was he? Didn't he know Field Marshalls were collectors' items?

"Can we help you?" she asked.

"I hope so." He consulted his clipboard again. "I'm looking for Arthur Roberts."

"Who shall I say is calling?"

"Just get him for me, will you?"

They all spoke at the same time.

"He's out," said Hannah.

"He's milking," said Jo.

"He's in the office," said Sam.

"I see," said the stranger. "Busy man."

They nodded.

"Well, is your mum in then?"

They were silent. Hannah had already seen quite enough of this stranger and she didn't want him to know any more about their lives than he did already. What else was written on that clipboard?

Along the lane a bell sounded. Hannah looked up. Lottie Perfect was bumping up the track on her brand-new bicycle, weaving around the puddles and potholes.

"Can I take a message?" Hannah asked. She had to get rid of him. She needed every second of her time with Lottie.

"Give your dad this," he said. "Make sure he gets it."

Hannah took the envelope. Printed across the top were the words "Strickland and Wormwood, Land Agents". And then, in red capital letters, "URGENT".

Thank goodness she hadn't called Dad. This man must be the agent for the new landlord. Hannah pulled on her coat and stuffed the letter and her script into one of the pockets.

The agent strutted off. Lottie, waving at Hannah from her bike, almost ran into him. She swerved wildly through a puddle. The children stared open-mouthed as a great brown wave of muddy water splattered all over the man's trousers. Sam giggled, and that made his sisters laugh too. The agent glared at them as he opened his car door, and they laughed even more.

Lottie braked at the garden gate. She jumped off her bike and yanked the gate open. "Look at the state of me," she said. "Have you got something to wipe this mud off, Han?"

"Right, you lazy lot!" shouted Dad down the stairs. "Look sharp!"

Oh, no, thought Hannah. If she got caught up in Dad's pig chase, she'd be gone all afternoon and they'd never get the play done.

She threw Lottie a threadbare towel from the draining board, then grabbed Jo's arm and pulled her outside, around the corner of the house. The guinea pig scrabbled across Jo's jumper.

"Hey, careful with Carrots!"

"Jo, you have to cover for me. *Please*. I've got to read through the play with Lottie. We need to make sure it's right so she can type it up. The competition closes on Tuesday – we have to send it off tomorrow."

"Oooh, I've got to read my play with Perfect Lottie," said Martha in a high-pitched singsong voice. "As if you'd win a prize with your stupid play."

Hannah swung round. "Martha, get lost. It's none of your business."

"Like I care anyway," said Martha. She stuck out her tongue at Hannah and teetered back inside.

Hannah turned to Jo. "Just tell him you don't know where I am. Please, Jo. I've *got* to do this play – if we win, it actually goes on the radio and it might be my chance to be an actress!"

Dad's heavy tread sounded from the stairs.

"I won't tell," said Jo. She placed Carrots in his hutch, sat on the scullery step and tugged on her muddy wellingtons. "Come on, Sam. Let's get your boots on."

Hannah skulked around the corner. Dad strode out into the yard with Sam trotting beside him. Jo followed them. And, finally, Martha emerged.

"Martha, please don't tell him! I'll give you anything!"

Martha shot her a contemptuous glance. "Like you've got anything I'd want."

She kicked off the red stilettos and rammed her feet into an old pair of Jo's boots. They were so much too small for her that she had to walk on tiptoe in them.

She staggered into the farmyard. "Dad, wait up!"

Dad was a good ten metres ahead of her and walking twice as fast. Hannah was spared. But not for long.